WIT

An extra-terrestrial sells porno-graphic literature from *his* world on Earth.

IMAGINATION

A politician seeks complete security, only to find . . .

CHARM

Modern art gets viewed from the future.

IRONY

Just what kind of an animal is a human being?

BY
WILLIAM
TENN

Of All Possible Worlds

The Human Angle

This is an original collection—not a reprint—
published by BALLANTINE BOOKS, INC.

THE
HUMAN ANGLE

WILLIAM TENN

Ballantine Books • **New York**

"Party of the Two Parts" and "Project Hush" (the latter in a different version) appeared in *Galaxy Science Fiction*, both Copyright 1954 by Galaxy Publishing Corporation; "The Discovery of Morniel Mathaway," "The Servant Problem," and "The Flat-Eyed Monster" appeared in *Galaxy Science Fiction*, Copyright 1955 by Galaxy Publishing Corporation; "Wednesday's Child" appeared in *Fantastic Universe*, Copyright 1955 by King-Size Publications, Inc.; "The Human Angle" appeared in *Famous Fantastic Mysteries*, Copyright 1948 by All-Fiction Field, Inc.

First printing: August, 1956
Second printing: April, 1964

Library of Congress Catalog Card No. 56-11224
Printed in the United States of America

Ballantine Books are distributed in the U. S. A. by Affiliated Publishers, a division of Pocket Books, Inc., 630 Fifth Avenue, New York 20, N. Y.

BALLANTINE BOOKS, INC.
101 Fifth Avenue • New York 3, N. Y.

Contents

Project Hush   1

The Discovery of Morniel Mathaway   7

Wednesday's Child   23

The Servant Problem   44

Party of the Two Parts   75

The Flat-Eyed Monster   98

The Human Angle   132

A Man of Family   137

PROJECT HUSH

SECRET? We were about as secret as you could be and still exist. Listen, do you know the name of our official listing in Army documents?

Project Hush.

You can imagine. Or, come to think of it, you really can't. Of course, everyone remembers the terrific espionage fever that gripped this country in the late nineteen-sixties, how every official named Tom had another official named Dick checking up on him, how Dick had someone named Harry checking up on *him*—and how Harry didn't have the slightest idea of the work Tom was doing because there was a limit as to how far you could trust even counter-intelligence men . . .

But you had to be in a top-secret Army project to really get it. Where a couple of times a week you reported to Psycho for DD and HA (Dream Detailing and Hypno-Analysis to you carefree civilians). Where even the commanding general of the heavily fortified research post to which you were assigned could not ask what the hell you were doing, under penalty of court-martial—and was supposed to shut his imagination off like a faucet every time he heard an explosion. Where your project didn't even appear in the military budget by name but under the classification *Miscellaneous X Research*—a heading that picked up a bigger appropriation every year like a runaway snowball. Where—

Oh, well, maybe you can still remember it. And, as I said, we were called Project *Hush*.

The goal of our project was not just to reach the moon and set up a permanent station there with an original complement of two men. That we had just done on that

1

slightly historic day of 24 June 1967. More important, in those wild, weapon-seeking times when fear of the H-bomb had churned the nation into a viscid mass of hysteria, was getting to the moon before anybody else and without anybody else knowing about it.

We'd landed at the northern tip of Mare Nubium, just off Regiomontanus, and, after planting a flag with appropriate throat-catching ceremony, had swung into the realities of the tasks we had practiced as so many dry runs back on earth.

Major Monroe Gridley prepared the big rocket, with its tiny cubicle of living space for the return journey to Earth which he alone would make.

Lieutenant-colonel Thomas Hawthorne painstakingly examined our provisions and portable quarters for any damage that might have been incurred in landing.

And I, Colonel Benjamin Rice, first commanding officer of Army Base No. 1 on the Moon, dragged crate after enormous crate out of the ship on my aching academic back, and piled them in the spot two hundred feet away where the plastic dome would be built.

We all finished at just about the same time, as per schedule, and went into Phase Two.

Monroe and I started work on building the dome. It was a simple pre-fab affair, but big enough to require an awful lot of assembling. Then, after it was built, we faced the real problem—getting all the complex internal machinery in place and in operating order.

Meanwhile, Tom Hawthorne took his plump self off in the single-seater rocket which, up to then, had doubled as a lifeboat.

The schedule called for him to make a rough three-hour scouting survey in an ever-widening spiral from our dome. This had been regarded as a probable waste of time, rocket fuel and manpower—but a necessary precaution. He was supposed to watch for such things as bug-eyed monsters out for a stroll on the Lunar landscape. Basically, however, Tom's survey was intended to supply extra geological and astronomical meat for the report which Monroe was to carry back to Army HQ on earth.

2

Tom was back in forty minutes. His round face, inside its transparent bubble helmet, was fishbelly white. And so were ours, once he told us what he'd seen.

He had seen another dome.

"The other side of Mare Nubium—in the Riphaen Mountains," he babbled excitedly. "It's a little bigger than ours, and it's a little flatter on top. And it's not translucent, either, with splotches of different colors here and there—it's a dull, dark, heavy gray. But that's all there is to see."

"No markings on the dome?" I asked worriedly. "No signs of anyone—or anything—around it?"

"Neither, Colonel." I noticed he was calling me by my rank for the first time since the trip started, which meant he was saying in effect, "Man, have *you* got a decision to make!"

"Hey, Tom," Monroe put in. "Couldn't be just a regularly shaped bump in the ground, could it?"

"I'm a geologist, Monroe, I can distinguish artificial from natural topography. Besides—" He looked up—"I just remembered something I left out. There's a brand-new tiny crater near the dome—the kind usually left by a rocket exhaust."

"Rocket exhaust?" I seized on that. "*Rockets*, eh?"

Tom grinned a little sympathetically. "Spaceship exhaust, I should have said. You can't tell from the crater what kind of propulsive device these characters are using. It's not the same kind of crater our rear-jets leave, if that helps any."

Of course it didn't. So we went into our ship and had a council of war. And I do mean war. Both Tom and Monroe were calling me Colonel in every other sentence. I used their first names every chance I got.

Still, no one but me could reach a decision. About what to do, I mean.

"Look," I said at last, "here are the possibilities. They know we are here—either from watching us land a couple of hours ago or from observing Tom's scoutship—or they do not know we are here. They are either humans from Earth—in which case they are in all probability enemy nationals—or they are alien creatures from another

3

planet—in which case they may be friends, enemies or what-have-you. I think common sense and standard military procedure demand that we consider them hostile until we have evidence to the contrary. Meanwhile, we proceed with extreme caution, so as not to precipitate an interplanetary war with potentially friendly Martians, or whatever they are.

"All right. It's vitally important that Army Headquarters be informed of this immediately. But since Moon-to-Earth radio is still on the drawing boards, the only way we can get through is to send Monroe back with the ship. If we do, we run the risk of having our garrison force, Tom and me, captured while he's making the return trip. In that case, their side winds up in possession of important information concerning our personnel and equipment, while our side has only the bare knowledge that somebody or something else has a base on the Moon. So our primary need is more information.

"Therefore, I suggest that I sit in the dome on one end of a telephone hookup with Tom, who will sit in the ship, his hand over the firing button, ready to blast off for earth the moment he gets the order from me. Monroe will take the single-seater down to the Riphaen Mountains, landing as close to the other dome as he thinks safe. He will then proceed the rest of the way on foot, doing the best scouting job he can in a spacesuit.

"He will not use his radio, except for agreed-upon nonsense syllables to designate landing the single-seater, coming upon the dome by foot, and warning me to tell Tom to take off. If he's captured, remembering that the first purpose of a scout is acquiring and transmitting knowledge of the enemy, he will snap his suit radio on full volume and pass on as much data as time and the enemy's reflexes permit. How does that sound to you?"

They both nodded. As far as they were concerned, the command decision had been made. But I was sitting under two inches of sweat.

"One question," Tom said. "Why did you pick Monroe for the scout?"

"I was afraid you'd ask that," I told him. "We're three extremely unathletic Ph. D.s who have been in the Army

4

since we finished our schooling. There isn't too much choice. But I remembered that Monroe is half Indian—Arapahoe, isn't it, Monroe?—and I'm hoping blood will tell."

"Only trouble, Colonel," Monroe said slowly as he rose, "is that I'm one-*fourth* Indian and even that . . . Didn't I ever tell you that my great-grandfather was the only Arapahoe scout who was with Custer at the Little Big Horn? He'd been positive Sitting Bull was miles away. However, I'll do my best. And if I heroically don't come back, would you please persuade the Security Officer of our section to clear my name for use in the history books? Under the circumstances, I think it's the least he could do."

I promised to do my best, of course.

After he took off, I sat in the dome over the telephone connection to Tom and hated myself for picking Monroe to do the job. But I'd have hated myself just as much for picking Tom. And if anything happened and I had to tell Tom to blast off, I'd probably be sitting here in the dome all by myself after that, waiting . . .

"*Broz neggle!*" came over the radio in Monroe's resonant voice. He had landed the single-seater.

I didn't dare use the telephone to chat with Tom in the ship, for fear I might miss an important word or phrase from our scout. So I sat and sat and strained my ears. After a while, I heard "*Mishgashu!*" which told me that Monroe was in the neighborhood of the other dome and was creeping toward it under cover of whatever boulders were around.

And then, abruptly, I heard Monroe yell my name and there was a terrific clattering in my headphones. Radio interference! He'd been caught, and whoever had caught him had simultaneously jammed his suit transmitter with a larger transmitter from the alien dome.

Then there was silence.

After a while, I told Tom what had happened. He just said, "Poor Monroe." I had a good idea of what his expression was like.

"Look, Tom," I said, "if you take off now, you still

5

won't have anything important to tell. After capturing Monroe whatever's in that other dome will come looking for us, I think. I'll let them get close enough for us to learn something of their appearance—at least if they're human or non-human. Any bit of information about them is important. I'll shout it up to you and you'll still be able to take off in plenty of time. All right?"

"You're the boss, Colonel," he said in a mournful voice. "Lots of luck."

And then there was nothing to do but wait. There was no oxygen system in the dome yet, so I had to squeeze up a sandwich from the food compartment in my suit. I sat there, thinking about the expedition. Nine years, and all that careful secrecy, all that expenditure of money and mind-cracking research—and it had come to this. Waiting to be wiped out, in a blast from some unimaginable weapon. I understood Monroe's last request. We often felt we were so secret that our immediate superiors didn't even want *us* to know what we were working on. Scientists are people—they wish for recognition, too. I was hoping the whole expedition would be written up in the history books, but it looked unpromising.

Two hours later, the scout ship landed near the dome. The lock opened and, from where I stood in the open door of our dome, I saw Monroe come out and walk toward me.

I alerted Tom and told him to listen carefully. "It may be a trick—he might be drugged . . ."

He didn't act drugged, though—not exactly. He pushed his way past me and sat down on a box to one side of the dome. He put his booted feet up on another, smaller box.

"How are you, Ben?" he asked. "How's every little thing?"

I grunted. "*Well?*" I know my voice skittered a bit.

He pretended puzzlement. "Well *what?* Oh, I see what you mean. The other dome—you want to know who's in it. You have a right to be curious, Ben. Certainly. The leader of a top-secret expedition like this—Project Hush they call us, huh, Ben—finds another dome on the Moon.

6

He thinks he's been the first to land on it, so naturally he wants to—"

"Major Monroe Gridley!" I rapped out. "You will come to attention and deliver your report. Now!" Honestly, I felt my neck swelling up inside my helmet.

Monroe just leaned back against the side of the dome. "That's the *Army* way of doing things," he commented admiringly. "Like the recruits say, there's a right way, a wrong way and an Army way. Only there are other ways, too." He chuckled. "Lots of other ways."

"He's off," I heard Tom whisper over the telephone. "Ben, Monroe has gone and blown his stack."

"They aren't extraterrestrials in the other dome, Ben," Monroe volunteered in a sudden burst of sanity. "No, they're humans, all right, and from Earth. Guess *where*."

"I'll kill you," I warned him. "I swear I'll kill you, Monroe. Where are they from—Russia, China, Argentina?"

He grimaced. "What's so secret about those places? Go on!—guess again."

I stared at him long and hard. "The only place else—"

"Sure," he said. "You got it, Colonel. The other dome is owned and operated by the Navy. The goddamn United States Navy!"

THE DISCOVERY
OF MORNIEL MATHAWAY

EVERYONE is astonished at the change in Morniel Mathaway since he was discovered, everyone but me. They remember him as an unbathed and untalented Greenwich Village painter who began almost every second sentence with "I" and ended every third one with "me." He had all the pushing, half-frightened conceit of the man who secretly suspects himself to be a second-rater or worse, and any half-hour conversation with him made your ears droop with the boastful yells he threw at them.

I understand the change in him, the soft-spoken self-depreciation as well as the sudden overwhelming success. But then, I was there the day he was "discovered"—except that isn't the right way to put it. To tell you the truth, I don't know how to put it really, considering the absolute impossibility—yes, I said *impossibility*, not improbability—of the whole business. All I know for sure is that trying to make sense out of it gives me belly-yammers and the biggest headache this side of calculus.

We were talking about his discovery that day. I was sitting, carefully balanced, on the one wooden chair in his cold little Bleecker Street studio, because I was too sophisticated to sit in the easy chair.

Morniel practically paid the rent on his studio with that easy chair. It was a broken-down tangle of filthy upholstery that was high in the front of the seat and very low in the back. When you sat in it, things began sliding out of your pockets—loose change, keys, wallets, anything—and into the jungle of rusty springs and rotting woodwork below.

Whenever newcomers came to the place, Morniel would make a big fuss about showing them to "the *comfortable* chair." And as they twisted about painfully trying to find a spot between the springs, his eyes would gleam and he'd get all lit up with good cheer. Because the more they moved about, the more would fall out of their pockets.

After a party, he'd take the chair apart and start counting the receipts, like a store owner hitting the cash register the evening after a fire sale.

The only trouble was, to sit in the wooden chair, you had to concentrate, since it teetered.

Morniel couldn't lose—he always sat on the bed.

"I can't wait for the day," he was saying, "when some dealer, some critic, with an ounce of brain in his head sees my work. I can't miss, Dave, I know I can't miss; I'm just too good. Sometimes I get frightened at how good I am—it's almost too much talent for one man."

"Well," I said, "there's always the—"

"Not that it's too much talent for me," he went on, fearful that I might have misunderstood him. "I'm big enough to carry it, fortunately; I'm large enough of soul. But another, lesser guy would be destroyed by this much totality of perception, this comprehension of the spiritual *gestalt* as I like to put it. His mind would just crack wide open under the load. Not me, though, Dave, not me."

"Good," I said. "Glad to hear it. Now if you don't m—"

"Do you know what I was thinking about this morning?"

"No," I said. "But, to tell you the truth, I don't really—"

"I was thinking about Picasso, Dave. Picasso and Roualt. I'd just gone for a walk through the pushcart area to have my breakfast—you know, the old the-hand-is-quicker-than-the-eye Morniel—and I started to think about the state of modern painting. I think about that a lot, Dave. It troubles me."

"You do?" I said. "Well, *I* tend to—"

"I walked down Bleecker Street, then I swung into Washington Square Park, and while I walked, I was thinking: Who is doing really important work in painting today who is really and unquestionably great? I could think of only three names: Picasso, Roualt—and me. There's nobody else doing anything worthwhile and original nowadays. Just three names out of the whole host of people painting all over the world at this moment: just three names, no more. It made me feel very lonely, Dave."

"I can see that," I said. "But then, you—"

"And then I asked myself, why is this so? Has absolute genius always been so rare, is there an essential statistical limitation on it in every period, or is there another reason, peculiar to our own time. And why has my impending discovery been delayed so long? I thought about it for a long time, Dave. I thought about it humbly, carefully, because it's an important question. And this is the answer I came up with."

I gave up. I just sat back in my chair—not too far back, of course—and listened to him expound a theory of esthetics I'd heard at least a dozen times before, from a dozen other painters in the Village. The only point of difference between them was on the question of exactly

9

who was the culmination and the most perfect living example of this esthetic. Morniel, you will probably not be amazed to learn, felt it was himself.

He'd come to New York from Pittsburgh, Pennsylvania, a tall, awkward boy who didn't like to shave and believed he could paint. In those days, he admired Gauguin and tried to imitate him on canvas; he'd talk for hours, in the accents that sound like movie Brooklynese, but are actually pure Pittsburgh, about the *mystique* of folk simplicity.

He got off the Gauguin kick fast, once he'd taken a few courses at the Art Students League and grown his first straggly blond beard. Recently, he had developed his own technique which he called smudge-on-smudge.

He was bad, and there were no two ways about it. I say that not only from my opinion—and I've roomed with two modern painters and been married for a year to another—but from the opinions of pretty knowing people who, having no personal axe to grind, looked his work over carefully.

One of them, a fine critic of modern art, said after staring slack-jawed at a painting which Morniel had insisted on giving me and which, in spite of my protests, he had personally hung over my fireplace: "It's not just that he doesn't say anything of any significance, graphically, but he doesn't even set himself what you might call *painterly* problems. White-on-white smudge-on-smudge, non-objectivism, neo-abstractionism, call it what you like, there's nothing there, nothing! He's just another of these loudmouth, frowzy, frustrated dilettantes that infest the Village."

So why did I spend time with Morniel? Well, he lived right around the corner. He was slightly colorful, in his own sick way. And when I'd sat up all night, trying to work on a poem that simply wouldn't be worked, I often felt it would be relaxing to drift around to his studio for a spot of conversation that wouldn't have anything to do with literature.

The only trouble—and the thing I always forgot—was that it almost never was a conversation. It was a monologue that I barely managed to break in on from time to time.

You see, the difference between us was that I'd been published, even if it was only in badly printed experimental magazines that paid off in subscriptions. He'd never been exhibited—not once.

There was another reason for my maintaining a friendly relationship with the man. And that had to do with the one talent he really had.

I barely get by, so far as living expenses are concerned. Things like good paper to write on, fine books for my library, are stuff I yearn for all the time, but are way out of my reach financially. When the yearning gets too great—for a newly published collection by Wallace Stevens, for example—I meander over to Morniel's and tell him about it.

Then we go out to the bookstore—entering it separately. I start a conversation with the proprietor about some very expensive, out-of-print item that I'm thinking of ordering and, once I've got all of his attention, Morniel snaffles the Stevens—which I intend to pay for, of course, as soon as I'm a little ahead.

He's absolutely wonderful at it. I've never seen him so much as suspected, let alone caught. Of course, I have to pay for the favor by going through the same routine in an art-supply store, so that Morniel can replenish his stock of canvas, paint and brushes, but it's worth it to me in the long run. The only thing it's not worth is the thumping boredom I have to suffer through in listening to the guy, or my conscience bothering me because I know he never intends to pay for those things. Okay, so I will, when I can.

"I can't be as unique as I feel I am," he was saying now. "Other people must be born with the potential of such great talent, but it's destroyed in them before they can reach artistic maturity. Why? How? Well, let's examine the role that society—"

And that's exactly when I first saw it. Just as he got to the word "society," I saw this purplish ripple in the wall opposite me, the strange, shimmering outline of a box with a strange, shimmering outline of a man inside the box.

It was about five feet off the floor and it looked like colored heat waves. Then there was nothing on the wall.

But it was too late in the year for heat waves. And I've never had optical illusions. It could be, I decided, that I had seen the beginnings of a new crack in Morniel's wall. The place wasn't really a studio, just a drafty cold-water flat that some old occupant had cleared so as to make one long room. It was on the top floor and the roof leaked occasionally; the walls were covered with thick, wavy lines in memory of the paths followed by the trickling water.

But why purple? And why the outline of a man inside a box? That was pretty tricky, for a simple crack in the wall. And where had it gone?

"—the eternal conflict with the individual who insists on his individuality," Morniel pointed out. "Not to mention—"

A series of high musical notes sounded, one after the other, rapidly. And then, in the center of the room, about two feet above the floor this time, the purple lines reappeared—still hazy, still transparent and still with the outline of a man inside.

Morniel swung his feet off the bed and stared up at it. "What the—" he began.

Once more, the outfit disappeared.

"W-what—" Morniel stuttered. "What's going *on?*"

"I don't know," I told him. "But whatever it is, I'd say they're slowly zeroing in."

Again those high musical notes. And the purple box came into view with its bottom resting on the floor. It got darker, darker and more substantial. The notes kept climbing up the scale and getting fainter and fainter until, when the box was no longer transparent, they faded away altogether.

A door slid back in the box. A man stepped out, wearing clothing that seemed to end everywhere in curlicues.

He looked first at me, then at Morniel.

"Morniel Mathaway?" he inquired.

"Ye-es," Morniel said, backing away toward his refrigerator.

"Morniel Mathaway," the man from the box said, "my

name is Glescu. I bring you greetings from 2487 A.D."

Neither of us could think of a topper for that one, so we let it lie there. I got up and stood beside Morniel, feeling obscurely that I wanted to get as close as possible to something I was familiar with.

And we all held that position for a while. Tableau.

I thought to myself, 2487 A.D. I'd never seen anyone dressed like that. Even more, I'd never *imagined* anyone dressed like that and my imagination can run pretty wild. The clothing was not exactly transparent and yet not quite opaque. Prismatic is the word for it, different colors that constantly chased themselves in and out and around the curlicues. There seemed to be a pattern to it, but nothing that my eyes could hold down and identify.

And the man himself, this Mr. Glescu, was about the same height as Morniel and me and he seemed to be not very much older. But there was a something about him—I don't know, call it *quality*, true and tremendous *quality* —that would have cowed the Duke of Wellington. Civilized, maybe that's the word: he was the most civilized-looking man I'd ever seen.

He stepped forward. "We will now," he said in a rich, wonderfully resonant voice, "indulge in the twentieth-century custom of shaking hands."

So we indulged in the twentieth-century custom of shaking hands with him. First Morniel, then me—and both very gingerly. Mr. Glescu shook hands with a peculiar awkwardness that made me think of the way an Iowan farmer might eat with chopsticks for the first time.

The ceremony over, he stood there and beamed at us. Or, rather, at Morniel.

"What a moment, eh?" he said. "What a supreme moment!"

Morniel took a deep breath and I knew that all those years of meeting process servers unexpectedly on the stairs had begun to pay off. He was recovering; his mind was beginning to work again.

"How do you mean 'what a moment'?" he asked. "What's so special about it? Are you the—the inventor of time travel?"

Mr. Glescu twinkled with laughter. "*Me? An inventor?*

13

Oh, no. No, no! Time travel was invented by Antoinette Ingeborg in—but that was after your time. Hardly worth going into at the moment, especially since I only have half an hour."

"Why half an hour?" I asked, not so much because I was curious as because it seemed like a good question.

"The skindrom can only be maintained that long," he elucidated. "The skindrom is—well, call it a transmitting device that enables me to appear in your period. There is such an enormous expenditure of power required that a trip into the past is made only once every fifty years. The privilege is awarded as a sort of Gobel. I hope I have the word right. It *is* Gobel isn't it? The award made in your time?"

I had a flash. "You wouldn't mean *Nobel*, by any chance? The Nobel Prize?"

He nodded his head enthusiastically. "That's it! The Nobel Prize. The trip is awarded to outstanding scholars as a kind of Nobel Prize. Once every fifty years—the man selected by the gardunax as the most pre-eminent—that sort of thing. Up to now, of course, it's always gone to historians and they've frittered it away on the Siege of Troy, the first atom-bomb explosion at Los Alamos, the discovery of America—things like that. But *this* year—"

"Yes?" Morniel broke in, his voice quavering. We were both suddenly remembering that Mr. Glescu had known his name. "What kind of scholar are you?"

Mr. Glescu made us a slight bow with his head, "I am an art scholar. My specialty is art history. And my special field in art history is . . ."

"*What?*" Morniel demanded, his voice no longer quavering, but positively screechy. "What is your special field?"

Again a slight bow from Mr. Glescu's head. "You, Mr. Mathaway. In my own period, I may say without much fear of contradiction, I am the greatest living authority on the life and works of Morniel Mathaway. My special field is you."

Morniel went white. He groped his way to the bed and sat down as if his hips were made of glass. He opened his mouth several times and couldn't seem to get a sound

14

out. Finally, he gulped, clenched his fists and got a grip on himself.

"Do—do you mean," he managed to croak at last, "that I'm famous? *That* famous?"

"Famous? You, my dear sir, are beyond fame. You are one of the immortals the human race has produced. As I put it—rather well if I may say so—in my last book, *Mathaway, the Man Who Shaped the Future:* 'How rarely has it fallen to the lot of individual human endeavor to—' "

"That famous." The blond beard worked the way a child's face does when it's about to cry. "*That* famous!"

"That famous!" Mr. Glescu assured him. "Who is the man with whom modern painting, in its full glory, is said to have definitely begun? Who is the man whose designs and special manipulations of color have dominated architecture for the past five centuries, who is responsible for the arrangement of our cities, the shape of our every artifact, the very texture of our clothing."

"Me?" Morniel inquired weakly.

"You!" No other man in the history of art has exerted such a massive influence over design or over so wide an area of art for so long a period of time. To whom can I compare you, sir? To what other artist in history can I compare you?"

"Rembrandt?" Morniel suggested. He seemed to be trying to be helpful. "Da Vinci?"

Mr. Glescu sneered. "Rembrandt and Da Vinci in the same breath as you? Ridiculous! They lacked your universality, your taste for the cosmic, your sense of the all-encompassing. No, to relate you properly to an equal, one must go outside painting, to literature, possibly. Shakespeare, with his vast breadth of understanding, with the resounding organ notes of his poetry and with his tremendous influence on the later English language—but even Shakespeare, I'm afraid, even Shakespeare—" He shook his head sadly.

"Wow!" breathed Morniel Mathaway.

"Speaking of Shakespeare," I broke in, "do you happen to know of a poet named David Dantziger? Did much of his work survive?"

"Is that you?"

15

"Yes," I told the man from 2487 A.D. eagerly. "That's me, Dave Dantziger."

He wrinkled his forehead. "I don't seem to remember any—What school of poetry do you belong to?"

"Well, they call it by various names. Anti-imagist is the most usual one. Anti-imagist or post-imagist."

"No," said Mr. Glescu after thinking for a while. "The only poet I can remember for this time and this part of the world is Peter Tedd."

"Who is Peter Tedd? Never heard of him."

"Then this must be before he was discovered. But please remember, I am an art scholar, not a literary one. It is entirely possible," he went on soothingly, "that were you to mention your name to a specialist in the field of minor twentieth-century versifiers, he could place you with a minimum of difficulty. Entirely possible."

I glanced at Morniel, and he was grinning at me from the bed. He had entirely recovered by now and was beginning to soak the situation in through his pores. The whole situation. His standing. Mine.

I decided I hated every single one of his guts.

Why did it have to be someone like Morniel Mathaway that got that kind of nod from fate? There were so many painters who were decent human beings, and yet this bragging slug . . .

And all the time, a big part of my mind was wandering around in circles. It just proved, I kept saying to myself, that you need the perspective of history to properly evaluate anything in art. You think of all the men who were big guns in their time and today are forgotten—that contemporary of Beethoven's, for example, who, while he was alive, was considered much the greater man, and whose name is known today only to musicologists. But still—

Mr. Glescu glanced at the forefinger of his right hand where a little black dot constantly expanded and contracted. "My time is getting short," he said. "And while it is an ineffable, overwhelming delight for me to be standing in your studio, Mr. Mathaway, and looking at you at last in the flesh, I wonder if you would mind obliging me with a small favor?"

16

"Sure," Morniel nodded, getting up. "You name it. Nothing's too good for you. What do you want?"

Mr. Glescu swallowed as if he were about to bring himself to knock on the gates of Paradise. "I wonder—I'm sure you don't mind—could you possibly let me look at the painting you're working on at the moment? The idea of seeing a Mathaway in an unfinished state, with the paint still wet upon it—" He shut his eyes, as if he couldn't believe that all this was really happening to him.

Morniel gestured urbanely and strode to his easel. He pulled the tarp off. "I intend to call this—" and his voice had grown as oily as the subsoil of Texas—"*Figured Figurines No. 29.*"

Slowly, tastingly, Mr. Glescu opened his eyes and leaned forward. "But—" he said, after a long silence. "Surely this isn't *your work*, Mr. Mathaway?"

Morniel turned around in surprise and considered the painting. "It's my work, all right. *Figured Figurines No. 29.* Recognize it?"

"No," said Mr. Glescu. "I do not recognize it. And that is a fact for which I am extremely grateful. Could I see something else, please? Something a little later?"

"That's the latest," Morniel told him a little uncertainly. "Everything else is earlier. Here, you might like this." He pulled a painting out of the rack. "I call this *Figured Figurines No. 22.* I think it's the best of my early period."

Mr. Glescu shuddered. "It looks like smears of paint on top of other smears of paint."

"Right! Only I call it smudge-on-smudge. But you probably know all that, being such an authority on me, And here's *Figured Figurines No. —*"

"Do you mind leaving these—these figurines, Mr. Mathaway?" Glescu begged. "I'd like to see something of yours with color. With color and with form!"

Morniel scratched his head. "I haven't done any real color work for a long time. Oh, wait!" he brightened and began to search in the back of the rack. He came out with an old canvas. "This is one of the few examples of my mauve-and-mottled period that I've kept."

"I can't imagine why," Mr. Glescu murmured, mostly to himself. "It's positively—" He brought his shoulders up to his ears in the kind of shrug that anyone who's ever seen an art critic in action can immediately recognize. You don't need words after that shrug; if you're a painter whose work he's looking at, you don't *want* words.

About this time, Morniel began pulling paintings out frantically. He'd show them to Glescu, who would gurgle as if he were forcing down a retch, and pull out some more paintings.

"I don't understand it," Mr. Glescu said, staring at the floor, which was strewn with canvases tacked to their wooden stretchers. "This was obviously before you discovered yourself and your true technique. But I'm looking for a sign, a *hint*, of the genius that is to come. And I find—" He shook his head dazedly.

"How about this one?" Morniel asked, breathing hard.

Mr. Glescu shoved at it with both hands. "Please take it *away!*" He looked at his forefinger again. I noticed the black dot was expanding and contracting much more slowly. "I'll have to leave soon," he said. "And I don't understand at all. Let me show you something, gentlemen."

He walked into the purple box and came out with a book. He beckoned to us. Morniel and I moved around behind him and stared over his shoulder The pages tinkled peculiarly as they were turned; one thing I knew for sure—they weren't made out of paper. And the title-page . . .

The Complete Paintings of Morniel Mathaway, 1928-1996.

"Were you born in 1928?" I demanded.

Morniel nodded. "May 23, 1928." And he was silent. I knew what he was thinking about and did a little quick figuring. Sixty-eight years. It's not given to many men to know exactly how much time they have. Sixty-eight years—that wasn't so bad.

Mr. Glescu turned to the first of the paintings.

Even now, when I remember my initial sight of it, my knees get weak and bend inward. It was an abstraction in full color, but such an abstraction as I'd never

18

imagined before. As if all the work of all the abstractionists up to this point had been an apprenticeship on the kindergarten level.

You had to like it—so long as you had eyes—whether or not your appreciation had been limited to representational painting until now; even if, in fact, you'd never particularly cared about painting of *any* school.

I don't want to sound maudlin, but I actually felt tears in my eyes. Anyone who was at all sensitive to beauty would have reacted the same way.

Not Morniel, though. "Oh, *that* kind of stuff," he said as if a great light had broken on him. "Why didn't you tell me you wanted *that* kind of stuff?"

Mr. Glescu clutched at Morniel's dirty tee-shirt. "Do you mean you have paintings like this, too?"

"Not paintings—*painting*. Just one. I did it last week as a sort of experiment, but I wasn't satisfied with the way it turned out, so I gave it to the girl downstairs. Care to take a look at it?"

"Oh, yes! Very, very much!"

Morniel reached for the book and tossed it casually on the bed. "Okay," he said. "Come on. It won't take more than a minute or two."

As we trooped downstairs, I found myself boiling with perplexity. One thing I was sure of—as sure as of the fact that Geoffrey Chaucer had lived before Algernon Swinburne—nothing that Morniel had ever done or had the capacity of ever doing could come within a million esthetic miles of the reproduction in that book. And for all of his boasting, for all of his seemingly inexhaustible conceit, I was certain that he also knew it.

He stopped before a door two floors below and rapped on it. There was no answer. He waited a few seconds and knocked again. Still no answer.

"Damn," he said. "She isn't home. And I did want you to see that one."

"I *want* to see it," Mr. Glescu told him earnestly. "I want to see anything that looks like your mature work. But time is growing so short—"

Morniel snapped his fingers. "Tell you what. Anita has a couple of cats she asks me to feed whenever she's away for a while, so she's given me a key to her apartment. Suppose I whip upstairs and get it?"

"Fine!" Mr. Glescu said happily, taking a quick look at his forefinger. "But please hurry."

"Will do." And then, as Morniel turned to go up the stairs, he caught my eye. And he gave me the signal, the one we use whenever we go "shopping." It meant: "Talk to the man. Keep him interested."

I got it. The book. I'd seen Morniel in action far too many times not to remember that casual gesture of tossing it on the bed as anything but a casual gesture. He'd just put it where he could find it when he wanted it—fast. He was going upstairs to hide it in some unlikely spot and when Mr. Glescu had to take off for his own time—well, the book would just not be available.

Smooth? Very pretty damned smooth, I'd say. And Morniel Mathaway would paint the paintings of Morniel Mathaway. Only he wouldn't paint them.

He'd *copy* them.

Meanwhile, the signal snapped my mouth open and automatically started me talking.

"Do you paint yourself, Mr. Glescu?" I asked. I knew that would be a good gambit.

"Oh, no! Of course, I wanted to be an artist when I was a boy—I imagine every critic starts out that way—and I even committed a few daubs of my own. But they were very bad, very bad indeed! I found it far easier to write about paintings than to do them. Once I began reading the life of Morniel Mathaway, I knew I'd found my field. Not only did I empathize closely with his paintings, but he seemed so much like a person I could have known and liked. That's one of the things that puzzles me. He's quite different from what I imagined."

I nodded. "I bet he is."

"Of course history has a way of adding stature and romance to any important figure. And I can see several things about his personality that the glamorizing process of the centuries could—but I shouldn't go on in this fashion, Mr. Dantziger. You're his friend."

"About as much of a friend as he's got in the world," I told him, "which isn't saying much."

And all the time I was trying to figure it out. But the more I figured, the more confused I got. The paradoxes in the thing. How could Morniel Mathaway become famous five hundred years from now by painting pictures that he first saw in a book published five hundred years from now? Who painted the pictures? Morniel Mathaway? The book said so, and with the book in his possession, he would certainly do them. But he'd be copying them out of the book. So who painted the original pictures?

Mr. Glescu looked worriedly at his forefinger. "I'm running out of time—practically none left!"

He sped up the stairs, with me behind him. When we burst into the studio, I braced myself for the argument over the book. I wasn't too happy about it, because I liked Mr. Glescu.

The book wasn't there; the bed was empty. And two other things weren't there—the time machine and Morniel Mathaway.

"He left in it!" Mr. Glescu gasped. "He *stranded* me here! He must have figured out that getting inside and closing the door made it return!"

"Yeah, he's a great figurer," I said bitterly. This I hadn't bargained for. This I wouldn't have helped to bring about. "And he'll probably figure out a very plausible story to tell the people in your time to explain how the whole thing happened. Why should he work his head off in the twentieth century when he can be an outstanding, hero-worshipped celebrity in the twenty-fifth?"

"But what will happen if they ask him to paint merely *one* picture—"

"He'll probably tell them he's already done his work and feels he can no longer add anything of importance to it. He'll no doubt end up giving lectures on himself. Don't worry, he'll make out. It's you I'm worried about. You're stuck here. Are they likely to send a rescue party after you?"

Mr. Glescu shook his head miserably. "Every scholar who wins the award has to sign a waiver of responsibility, in case he doesn't return. The machine may be used only once in fifty years—and by that time, some other scholar will claim and be given the right to witness the storming

21

of the Bastille, the birth of Gautama Buddha or something of the sort. No, I'm *stuck* here, as you phrased it. Is it very bad, living in this period?"

I slapped him on the shoulder. I was feeling very guilty. "Not so bad. Of course, you'll need a social security card, and I don't know how you go about getting one at your age. And possibly—I don't know for sure—the F.B.I. or immigration authorities may want to question you, since you're an illegal alien, kind of."

He looked appalled. "Oh, dear! That's quite bad enough!"

And then I got the idea. "No, it needn't be. Tell you what. Morniel has a social security card—he had a job a couple of years ago. And he keeps his birth certificate in that bureau drawer along with other personal papers. Why don't you just assume his identity? *He'll* never show you up as an imposter!"

"Do you think I could? Won't I be—won't his friends—his relatives—"

"Parents both dead, no relatives I ever heard about. And I told you I'm the closest thing to a friend he's got." I examined Mr. Glescu thoughtfully. "You could get away with it. Maybe grow a beard and dye it blond. Things like that. Naturally, the big problem would be earning a living. Being a specialist on Mathaway and the art movements that derived from him wouldn't get you fed an awful lot right now."

He grabbed at me. "I could paint! I've always dreamed of being a painter! I don't have much talent, but there are all sorts of artistic novelties I know about, all kinds of graphic innovations that don't exist in your time. Surely that would be enough—even without talent—to make a living for me on some third- or fourth-rate level!"

It was. It certainly was. But not on the third- or fourth-rate level. On the first. Mr. Glescu-Morniel Mathaway is the finest painter alive today. And the unhappiest.

"What's the matter with these people?" he asked me wildly after his last exhibition. "Praising me like that! I don't have an ounce of real talent in me; all my work, *all*, is completely derivative. I've tried to do something, *anything*, that was completely my own, but I'm so steeped

22

in Mathaway that I just can't seem to make my own personality come through. And those idiotic critics go on raving about me—and the work isn't even my own!"

"Then whose is it?" I wanted to know.

"Mathaway's, of course," he said bitterly. "We thought there couldn't be a time paradox—I wish you could read all the scientific papers on the subject; they fill whole libraries—because it isn't possible, the time specialists argue, for a painting, say, to be copied from a future reproduction and so have no original artist. But that's what I'm doing! I'm copying from that book by memory!"

I wish I could tell him the truth—he's such a nice guy, especially compared to the real fake of a Mathaway, and he suffers so much.

But I can't.

You see, he's deliberately trying not to copy those paintings. He's working so hard at it that he refuses to think about that book or even discuss it. I finally got him to recently, for a few sentences, and you know what? He doesn't actually remember, except pretty hazily!

Of course he wouldn't—he's the real Morniel Mathaway and there is no paradox. But if I ever told him that he was actually painting the pictures instead of merely copying them from memory, he'd lose whatever little self-confidence he has. So I have to let him think he's a phony when he's nothing of the sort.

"Forget it," I go on telling him. "A buck's a buck."

WEDNESDAY'S CHILD

WHEN HE FIRST CAME to scrutinize Wednesday Gresham with his rimless spectacles and watery blue eyes, Fabian Balik knew nothing of the biological contradictions which were so incredibly a part of her essential body structure. He had not even noticed—as yet—that she was a remarkably pretty girl with eyes like rain-sparkling violets. His original preoccupation with her was solely and specifically as a problem in personnel administration.

All of which was not too surprising, because Fabian Balik was a thoroughly intent, thoroughly sincere young office manager, who had convinced his glands conclusively, in several bitter skirmishes, that their interests didn't have a chance against the interests of SLAUGHTER, STARK & SLINGSBY: Advertising & Public Relations.

Wednesday was one of the best stenographers in the secretarial pool that was under his immediate supervision. There were, however, small but highly unusual derelictions in her employment history. They consisted of peculiarities which a less dedicated and ambitious personnel man might have put aside as mere trifles, but which Fabian, after a careful study of her six-year record with the firm, felt he could not, in good conscience, ignore. On the other hand, they would obviously require an extended discussion and he had strong views about cutting into an employee's working time.

Thus, much to the astonishment of the office and the confusion of Wednesday herself, he came up to her one day at noon, and informed her quite calmly that they were going to have lunch together.

"This is a nice place," he announced, when they had been shown to a table. "It's not too expensive, but I've discovered it serves the best food in the city for the price. And it's a bit off the beaten track so that it never gets too crowded. Only people who know what they want manage to come here."

Wednesday glanced around, and nodded. "Yes," she said. "I like it too. I eat here a lot with the girls."

After a moment, Fabian picked up a menu. "I suppose you don't mind if I order for both of us?" he inquired. "The chef is used to my tastes. He'll treat us right."

The girl frowned. "I'm terribly sorry, Mr. Balik, but—"

"Yes?" he said encouragingly, though he was more than a little surprised. He hadn't expected anything but compliance. After all, she was probably palpitating at being out with him.

"I'd like to order for myself," she said. "I'm on a - - a special diet."

He raised his eyebrows and was pleased at the way she blushed. He nodded slowly, with dignity, letting his displeasure come through in the way he pronounced his words. "Very well, as you please."

A few moments later, though, curiosity got too strong and broke through the ice. "What kind of diet is that? Fresh-fruit salad, a glass of tomato juice, raw cabbage, and a *baked potato?* You can't be trying to lose weight if you eat potatoes."

Wednesday smiled timidly. "I'm not trying to reduce, Mr. Balik. Those are all foods rich in Vitamin C. I need a lot of Vitamin C."

Fabian remembered her smile. There had been a few spots of more-than-natural whiteness in it. "Bad teeth?" he inquired.

"Bad teeth and—" Her tongue came out and paused for a thoughtful second between her lips. "Mostly bad teeth," she said. "This is a nice place. There's a restaurant almost like it near where I live. Of course it's a lot cheaper—"

"Do you live with your parents, Miss Gresham?"

"No, I live alone. I'm an orphan."

He waited until the waiter had deposited the first course, then speared a bit of the shrimp and returned to the attack. "Since when?"

She stared at him over her fresh-fruit salad. "I beg your pardon, Mr. Balik?"

"Since when? How long have you been an orphan?"

"Since I was a little baby. Someone left me on the doorstep of a foundling home."

He noticed that while she was replying to his questions in an even tone of voice, she was staring at her food with a good deal of concentration and her blush had become more pronounced. Was she embarrassed at having to admit her probable lack of legitimacy? he wondered. Surely she had grown accustomed to it in—how old was she?—twenty-four years. Nonsense, of course she had.

"But on your original application form, Miss Gresham, you gave Thomas and Mary Gresham as the names of your parents."

Wednesday had stopped eating and was playing with her water glass. "They were an old couple who adopted me," she said in a very low voice. "They died when I was fifteen. I have no living relatives."

"That you know of," he pointed out, raising a cautionary finger.

Much to Fabian's surprise she chuckled. It was a very odd chuckle and made him feel extremely uncomfortable. "That's right, Mr. Balik. I have no living relatives—*that I know of.*" She looked over his shoulder and chuckled again. "That I know of," she repeated softly to herself.

Fabian felt irritably that the interview was somehow getting away from him. He raised his voice slightly. "Then who is Dr. Morris Lorington?"

She was attentive again. In fact wary was more like it. "Dr. Morris Lorington?"

"Yes, the man you said should be notified in case of emergency. In case anything happened to you while you were working for us."

She looked very wary now. Her eyes were narrowed, she was watching him very closely; her breathing was a bit faster, too. "Dr. Lorington is an old friend. He—he was the doctor at the orphanage. After the Greshams adopted me, I kept going to him whenever—" Her voice trailed off.

"Whenever you needed medical attention?" Fabian suggested.

"Ye-es," she said, brightening, as if he had come up with an entirely novel reason for consulting a physician. "I saw him whenever I needed medical attention."

Fabian grunted. There was something very wrong but tantalizingly elusive about this whole business. But she was answering his questions. He couldn't deny that: she was certainly answering.

"Do you expect to see him next October?" he inquired.

And now Wednesday was no longer wary. She was frightened. "Next October?" she quavered.

Fabian finished the last of his shrimp and wiped his lips. But he didn't take his eyes off her. "Yes, next October, Miss Gresham. You've applied for a month's leave of absence, beginning October fifteenth. Five years ago, after you had been working for Slaughter, Stark and Slingsby for thirteen months, you also applied for a leave of absence in October."

He was amazed at how scared she looked. He felt triumphantly that he had been right in looking into this. The feeling he had about her had not been merely curiosity; it had been an instinct of good personnel management.

"But I'm not getting paid for the time off. I'm not asking to be paid for it, Mr. Balik. And I didn't get paid the —the other time."

She was clutching her napkin up near her face, and she gave the impression of being ready to bolt through the back door of the restaurant. Her blushes had departed with such thoroughness as to leave her skin absolutely white.

"The fact that you're not going to be paid for the time off, Miss Gresham—" Fabian began, only to be interrupted by the waiter with the entree. By the time the man had gone, he was annoyed to observe that Wednesday had used the respite to recover some of her poise. While she was still pale, she had a spot of red in each cheek and she was leaning back in her chair now instead of using the edge of it

"The fact that you're not going to be paid is of no consequence," he continued nonetheless. "It's merely logical. After all, you have two weeks of vacation with pay every year. Which brings me to the second point. You have every year made *two* unusual requests. First, you've asked for an additional week's leave of absence without pay, making three weeks in all. And then you've asked—"

"To take it in the early Spring," she finished, her voice entirely under control. "Is there anything wrong with that, Mr. Balik? That way I don't have any conflict with the other girls and the firm is sure of a secretary being in the office all through the summer."

"There's nothing wrong with that *per se*. By that I mean," he explained carefully, "that there is nothing wrong with the arrangement *as such*. But it makes for loose ends, for organizational confusion. And loose ends, Miss Gresham, loose ends and organizational confusion have no place in a well-regulated office."

He was pleased to note that she was looking uncomfortable again.

"Does that mean—are you trying to tell me that—I might be laid off?"

"It could happen," Fabian agreed, neglecting to add that it was, however, very unlikely to happen in the case of a secretary who was as generally efficient on the one hand, and as innocuous on the other, as Wednesday Gresham. He carefully cut a fork-sized portion of roast beef free of its accompanying strip of orange fat before going on; "Look at it this way. How would it be if every girl in the office asked for an additional week's leave of absence every year—even if it was without pay, as it would have to be? And then, every few years, wanted an additional month's leave of absence on top of that? What kind of an office would we have, Miss Gresham? Not a well-regulated one, certainly."

As he chewed the roast beef with the requisite thoroughness he beamed at the thoughtful concern on her face and was mentally grateful that he hadn't had to present that line of argument to anyone as sharp as Arlette Stein, for example. He knew what the well-hipped thirtyish widow would have immediately replied: "But every girl in the office *doesn't* ask for it, Mr. Balik." A heavy sneer at such sophistry would mean little to Stein.

Wednesday, he appreciated, was not the person to go in for such counterattacks. She was rolling her lips distressedly against each other and trying to think of a polite, good-employee way out. There was only one, and she would have to come to it in a moment.

She did.

"Would it help any," she began, and stopped. She took a deep breath. "Would it help any, if I told you the reasons—for the leaves-of-absence?"

"It would," he said heartily. "It would indeed, Miss Gresham. That way I, as office manager, can operate from facts instead of mysteries. I can hear your reasons, weigh them for validity and measure their importance—*and* your usefulness as a secretary—against the disorganization your absences create in the day-to-day operation of Slaughter, Stark and Slingsby."

28

"M-m-m." She looked troubled, uncertain. "I'd like to think a bit, if you don't mind."

Fabian waved a cauliflower-filled fork magnanimously. "Take all the time in the world! Think it out carefully. Don't tell me anything you aren't perfectly willing to tell me. Of course anything you *do* tell me will be, I am sure I need hardly reassure you, completely confidential. I will treat it as official knowledge, Miss Gresham—not personal. And while you're thinking, you might start eating your raw cabbage. Before it gets cold," he added with a rich, executive-type chuckle.

She nodded him a half-smile that ended in a sigh and began working at her plate in an absent-minded, not-particularly-hungry fashion.

"You see," she began abruptly as if she'd found a good point of departure, "some things happen to me that don't happen to other people."

"That, I would say, is fairly obvious."

"They're not bad things. I mean what, oh, the newspapers would call bad. And they're not dangerous things, exactly. They're—they're more physical-like. They're things that could happen to my body."

Fabian finished his plate, sat back and crossed his arms. "Could you be just a little more specific? Unless—" and he was struck by a horrifying thought—"unless they're what is known as, er, as *female* difficulties. In that case, of course—"

This time she didn't even blush. "Oh, no. Not at all. At least there's very little of that. It's—other things. Like my appendix. Every year I have to have my appendix out."

"Your appendix?" He turned that over in his mind. "Every year? But a human being only has one appendix. And once it's removed, it doesn't grow back."

"Mine does. On the tenth of April, every single year, I get appendicitis and have to have an operation. That's why I take my vacation then. And my teeth. Every five years, I lose all my teeth. I start losing them about this time, and I have dental plates that were made when I was a little girl—I use them until my teeth grow back. Then, about the middle of October, the last of them goes and new ones start coming up. I can't use my dental plates while they're growing, so I look kind of funny for a while. That's why I ask for a leave of absence. In the middle of November, the new teeth are almost full-grown, and I come back to work."

She took a deep breath and timidly lifted her eyes to his face. That was all she evidently had to say. Or wished to.

All through dessert, he thought about it. He was positive she was telling the truth. A girl like Wednesday Gresham didn't lie. Not to such a fantastic extent. Not to her boss.

"Well," he said at last. "It's certainly very unusual."

"Yes," she agreed. "Very unusual."

"Do you have anything else the matter with— I mean, are there any other peculiarities— Oh, darn! Is there anything else?"

Wednesday considered. "There are. But, if you don't mind, Mr. Balik, I'd rather not—"

Fabian decided not to take that. "Now see here, Miss Gresham," he said firmly. "Let us not play games. You didn't have to tell me anything, but you decided, for yourself, for your own good reasons, to do so. Now I must insist on the whole story, and nothing but the whole story. What other physical difficulties do you have?"

It worked. She cringed a bit in her chair, straightened up again, but a little weakly, and began: "I'm sorry, Mr. Balik, I wouldn't dream of—of playing games with you. There are lots of other things, but none of them interfere with my work, really. Like I have some tiny hairs growing on my fingernails. See?"

Fabian glanced at the hand held across the table. A few almost microscopic tendrils on each glittering hard surface of fingernail.

"What else?"

"Well, my tongue. I have a few hairs on the underside of my tongue. They don't bother me, though, they don't bother me in any way. And there's my—my—"

"Yes?" he prompted. *Who could believe that colorless little Wednesday Gresham . . .*

"My navel. I don't have any navel."

30

"You don't have any— But that's impossible!" he exploded. He felt his glasses sliding down his nose. "Everyone has a navel! Everyone alive—everyone who's ever been born."

Wednesday nodded, her eyes unnaturally bright and large. "Maybe—" she began, and suddenly, unexpectedly, broke into tears. She brought her hands up to her face and sobbed through them, great, pounding, wracking sobs that pulled her shoulders up and down, up and down.

Fabian's consternation made him completely helpless. He'd never, never in his life, been in a crowded restaurant with a crying girl before.

"Now, Miss Gresham—Wednesday," he managed to get out, and he was annoyed to hear a high, skittery note in his own voice. "There's no call for this. Surely, there's no call for this? Uh—Wednesday?"

"Maybe," she gasped again, between sobs, "m-maybe that's the answer."

"What's the answer?" Fabian asked loudly, desperately hoping to distract her into some kind of conversation.

"About—about being born. Maybe—maybe I wasn't born. M-maybe I was m-m-made!"

And then, as if she'd merely been warming up before this, she *really* went into hysterics. Fabian Balik at last realized what he had to do. He paid the check, put his arm around the girl's waist and half-carried her out of the restaurant.

It worked. She got quieter the moment they hit the open air. She leaned against a building, not crying now, and shook her shoulders in a steadily diminishing crescendo. Finally, she *ulped* once, twice, and turned groggily to him, her face looking as if it had been rubbed determinedly in an artist's turpentine rag.

"I'm s-sorry," she said. "I'm t-terribly s-sorry. I haven't done that for years. But—you see, Mr. Balik—I haven't talked about myself for years."

"There's a nice bar at the corner," he pointed out, tremendously relieved. She'd looked for a while as if she'd intended to keep on crying all day! "Let's pop in, and I'll have a drink. You can use the ladies' room to fix yourself up."

31

He took her arm and steered her into the place. Then he climbed onto a bar stool and had himself a double brandy.

What an experience! And what a strange, strange girl!

Of course, he shouldn't have pushed her quite so hard on a subject about which she was evidently so sensitive. Was that his fault, though, that she *was* so sensitive?

Fabian considered the matter carefully, judicially, and found in his favor. No, it definitely wasn't his fault.

But what a story! The foundling business, the appendix business, the teeth, the hair on the fingernails and tongue . . . And that last killer about the navel!

He'd have to think it out. And maybe he'd get some other opinions. But one thing he was sure of, as sure as of his own managerial capacities: Wednesday Gresham hadn't been lying in any particular. Wednesday Gresham was just not the sort of a girl who made up tall stories about herself.

When she rejoined him, he urged her to have a drink. "Help you get a grip on yourself."

She demurred, she didn't drink very much, she said. But he insisted, and she gave in. "Just a liqueur. Anything. You order it, Mr. Balik."

Fabian was secretly very pleased at her docility. No reprimanding, no back-biting, like most other girls— Although what in the world could she reprimand him for?

"You still look a little frayed," he told her. "When we get back, don't bother going to your desk. Go right in to Mr. Osborne and finish taking dictation. No point in giving the other girls something to talk about. I'll sign in for you."

She inclined her head submissively and continued to sip from the tiny glass.

"What was that last comment you made in the restaurant—I'm certain you don't mind discussing it, now— about not being born, but being made? That was an odd thing to say."

Wednesday sighed. "It isn't my own idea. It's Dr. Lorington's. Years ago, when he was examining me, he said that I looked as if I'd been made—by an amateur. By someone who didn't have all the blueprints, or didn't understand them, or wasn't concentrating hard enough."

"Hm." He stared at her, absolutely intrigued. She looked normal enough. Better than normal, in fact. And yet—

Later that afternoon, he telephoned Jim Rudd and made an appointment for right after work. Jim Rudd had been his roommate in college and was now a doctor: he would be able to tell him a little more about this.

But Jim Rudd wasn't able to help him very much. He listened patiently to Fabian's story about "a girl I've just met" and, at the end of it, leaned back in the new upholstered swivel chair and pursed his lips at his diploma, neatly framed and hung on the opposite wall.

"You sure do go in for weirdies, Fabe. For a superficially well-adjusted, well-organized guy with a real talent for the mundane things of life, you pick the damndest women I ever heard of. But that's your business. Maybe it's your way of adding a necessary pinch of the exotic to the grim daily round. Or maybe you're making up for the drabness of your father's grocery store."

"This girl is not a weirdie," Fabian insisted angrily. "She's a very simple little secretary, prettier than most, but that's about all."

"Have it your own way. To me, she's a weirdie. To me, there's not a hell of a lot of difference—from your description—between her and that crazy White Russian dame you were running around with back in our junior year. You know the one I mean—what was her name?"

"Sandra? Oh, Jim, what's the matter with you? Sandra was a bollixed-up box of dynamite who was always blowing up in my face. This kid turns pale and dies if I so much as raise my voice. Besides, I had a real puppy-love crush on Sandra; this other girl is somebody I just met, like I told you, and I don't feel anything for her, one way or the other."

The young doctor grinned. "So you come up to my office and have a consultation about her! Well, it's your funeral. What do you want to know?"

"What causes all these—these physical peculiarities?"

Dr. Rudd got up and sat on the edge of his desk. "First," he said, "whether you want to recognize it or not, she's a highly disturbed person. The hysterics in the restaurant

33

point to it, and the fantastic nonsense she told you about her body points to it. So right there, you have something. If only one per cent of what she told you is true—and even that I would say is pretty high—it makes sense in terms of psychosomatic imbalance. Medicine doesn't yet know quite how it works, but one thing seems certain: anyone badly mixed up mentally is going to be at least a little mixed up physically, too."

Fabian thought about that for a while. "Jim, you don't know what it means to those little secretaries in the pool to tell lies to the office manager! A fib or two about why they were absent the day before, yes, but not stories like this, not to *me*."

A shrug. "I don't know what you look like to them: I don't work for you, Fabe. But none of what you say would hold true for a psycho. And a psycho is what I have to consider her. Look, some of that stuff she told you is impossible, some of it has occurred in medical literature. There have been well-authenticated cases of people, for example, who have grown several sets of teeth in their lifetime. These are biological sports, one-in-a-million individuals. But the rest of it? And all the rest of it happening to one person? *Please*."

"I saw some of it. I saw the hairs on her fingernails."

"You saw something on her fingernails. It could be any one of a dozen different possibilities. I'm sure of one thing; it wasn't hair. Right there she gave herself away as phony. Goddammit, man, hair and nails are the same organs essentially. One doesn't grow on the other!"

"And the navel? The missing navel?"

Jim Rudd dropped to his feet and strode rapidly about the office. "I wish I knew why I'm wasting so much time with you," he complained. "A human being without a navel, or *any* mammal without a navel, is as possible as an insect with a body temperature of ninety-eight degrees. It just can't be. It does not exist."

He seemed to get more and more upset as he considered it. He kept shaking his head negatively as he walked.

Fabian suggested: "Suppose I brought her to your office. And suppose you examined her and found no navel.

Now just consider that for a moment. What would you say then?"

"I'd say plastic surgery," the doctor said instantly. "Mind you, I'm positive she'd never submit to such an examination, but if she did, and there was no navel, plastic surgery would be the only answer."

"Why would anyone want to do plastic surgery on a navel?"

"I don't know. I haven't the vaguest idea. Maybe an accident. Maybe a disfiguring birthmark in that place. But there will be scars, let me tell you. *She had to be born with a navel.*"

Rudd went back to his desk. He picked up a prescription pad. "Let me give you the name of a good psychiatrist, Fabe. I've thought ever since that Sandra business that you've had some personal problems that might get out of hand one day. This man is one of the finest—"

Fabian left.

She was obviously in a flutter when he called to pick her up that night, so much more of a flutter than a date-with-the-boss would account for, that Fabian was puzzled. But he waited and gave her an ostentatious and expensive good time. Afterward, after dinner and after the theater, when they were sitting in the corner of a small night club over their drinks, he asked her about it.

"You don't date much, do you, Wednesday?"

"No, I don't, Mr. Balik—I mean, Fabian," she said, smiling shyly as she remembered the first-name privilege she had been accorded for the evening. "I usually just go out with girl friends, not with men. I usually turn down dates."

"Why? You're not going to find a husband that way. You want to get married, don't you?"

Wednesday shook her head slowly. "I don't think so. I—I'm afraid to. Not of marriage. Of babies. I don't think a person like me ought to have a baby."

"Nonsense! Is there any scientific reason why you shouldn't? What are you afraid of—it'll be a monster?"

"I'm afraid it might be . . . anything. I think with my

body being as—as funny as it is, I shouldn't take chances with a child. Dr. Lorington thinks so too. Besides, there's the poem."

Fabian put down his drink. "Poem? What poem?"

"You know, the one about the days of the week. I learned it when I was a little girl, and it frightened me even then. It goes:

> *Monday's child is fair of face,*
> *Tuesday's child is full of grace,*
> *Wednesday's child is full of woe,*
> *Thursday's child has far to go,*
> *Friday's child is loving and giving—*

And so on. When I was a little girl in the orphanage, I used to say to myself, 'I'm Wednesday. I'm different from all other little girls in all kinds of strange ways. And my child—' "

"Who gave you that name?"

"I was left at the foundling home just after New Year's Eve—Wednesday morning. So they didn't know what else to call me, especially when they found I didn't have a navel. And then, like I told you, after the Greshams adopted me, I took their last name."

He reached for her hand and grasped it firmly with both of his. He noted with triumphant pleasure that her fingernails *were* hairy. "You're a very pretty girl, Wednesday Gresham."

When she saw that he meant it, she blushed and looked down at the tablecloth.

"And you really don't have a navel?"

"No, I don't. Really."

"What else about you is different?" Fabian asked. "I mean, besides the things you told me."

"Well," she considered. "There's that business about my blood pressure."

"Tell me about it," he urged.

She told him.

Two dates later, she informed Fabian that Dr. Lorington wanted to see him. Alone.

36

He went all the way uptown to the old-fashioned brownstone, chewing his knuckles in excitement. He had so many questions to ask!

Dr. Lorington was a tall, aged man with pale skin and absolutely white hair. He moved very slowly as he gestured his visitor to a chair, but his eyes rested intent and anxious on Fabian's face.

"Wednesday tells me you've been seeing a good deal of her, Mr. Balik. May I ask why?"

Fabian shrugged. "I like the girl. I'm interested in her."

"Interested, how? Interested clinically—as in a specimen?"

"What a way to put it, Doctor! She's a pretty girl, she's a nice girl, why should I be interested in her as a specimen?"

The doctor stroked an invisible beard on his chin, still watching Fabian very closely. "She's a pretty girl," he agreed, "but there are many pretty girls. You're a young man obviously on his way up in the world, and you're also obviously far out of Wednesday's class. From what she's told me—and mind you, it's been all on the positive side—I've gotten a definite impression that you look on her as a specimen, but a specimen, let us say, about which you feel a substantial collector's itch. Why you should feel this way, I don't know enough about you to say. But no matter how she rhapsodizes about you, I continue to feel strongly that you have no conventional, expected emotional interest in her. And now that I've seen you, I'm positive that this is so."

"Glad to hear she rhapsodizes about me." Fabian tried to squeeze out a bashful-type grin. "You have nothing to worry about, Doctor."

"I think there's quite a bit to worry about, quite a bit. Frankly, Mr. Balik, your appearance has confirmed my previous impressions: I am quite certain I don't like you. Furthermore, I don't like you for Wednesday."

Fabian thought for a moment, then shrugged. "That's too bad. But I don't think she'll listen to you. She's gone without male companionship too long, and she's too flattered by my going after her."

"I'm terribly afraid you're right. Listen to me, Mr.

Balik. I'm very fond of Wednesday and I know how un-guarded she is. I ask you, almost as a father, to leave her alone. I've taken care of her since she arrived at the found-ling home. I was responsible for keeping her case out of the medical journals so that she might have some chance for a normal life. At the moment, I'm retired from prac-tice. Wednesday Gresham is my only regular patient. Couldn't you find it in your heart to be kind and have nothing more to do with her?"

"What's this about her being made, not born?" Fabian countered. "She says it was your idea."

The old man sighed and shook his head over his desk-top for a long moment. "It's the only explanation that makes sense," he said at last, dispiritedly. "Considering the somatic inaccuracies and ambivalences."

Fabian clasped his hands and rubbed his elbows thought-fully on the arms of his chair. "Did you ever think there might be another explanation? She might be a mutant, a new kind of human evolution, or the offspring of crea-tures from another world, say, who happened to be stranded on this planet."

"Highly unlikely," Dr. Lorington said. "None of these physical modifications is especially useful in any con-ceivable environment, with the possible exception of the constantly renewing teeth. Nor are the modifications fatal. They tend to be just—inconvenient. As a physician who has examined many human beings in my life, I would say that Wednesday is thoroughly, indisputably human. She is just a little—well, the word is *amateurish*."

The doctor sat up straight. "There is something else, Mr. Balik. I think it extremely inadvisable for people like Wednesday to have children of their own."

Fabian's eyes lit up in fascination. "Why? What would the children be like?"

"They might be like anything imaginable—or unimag-inable. With so much disarrangement of the normal physi-cal system, the modification in the reproductive functions must be enormous too. That's why I ask you, Mr. Balik, not to go on seeing Wednesday, not to go on stimulating her to thoughts of marriage. Because this is one girl that I am certain should not have babies!"

38

"We'll see." Fabian rose and offered his hand. "Thank you very much for your time and trouble, Doctor."

Dr. Lorington cocked his head and stared up at him. Then, without shaking the hand, he said in a quiet, even voice. "You are welcome. Goodbye, Mr. Balik."

Wednesday was naturally miserable over the antagonism between the two men. But there was very little doubt where her loyalties would lie in a crisis. All those years of determined emotional starvation had resulted in a frantic voracity. Once she allowed herself to think of Fabian romantically, she was done for. She told him that she did her work at the office—from which their developing affair had so far been successfully screened—in a daze at the thought that *he* liked *her*.

Fabian found her homage delicious. Most women he had known began to treat him with a gradually sharpening edge of contempt as time went on. Wednesday became daily more admiring, more agreeable, more compliant.

True, she was by no means brilliant, but she was, he told himself, extremely pretty, and therefore quite presentable. Just to be on the safe side, he found an opportunity to confer with Mr. Slaughter, the senior partner of the firm, ostensibly on personnel matters. He mentioned in passing that he was slightly interested in one of the girls in the secretarial pool. Would there be any high-echelon objection to that?

"Interested to the extent of perhaps marrying the girl?" Mr. Slaughter asked, studying him from under a pair of enormously thick eyebrows.

"Possibly. It might very well come to that, sir. If you have no ob—"

"No objection at all, my boy, no objection at all! I don't like executives flim-flamming around with their file-clerks as a general rule, but if it's handled quietly and ends in matrimony, it could be an excellent thing for the office. I'd like to see you married, and steadied down. It might give the other single people in the place some sensible ideas for a change. But mind you, Balik, no flim-flam. No hanky-panky, especially on office time!"

Satisfied, Fabian now devoted himself to separating Wednesday from Dr. Lorington. He pointed out to her that the old man couldn't live much longer and she needed a regular doctor who was young enough to be able to help her with the physical complexities she faced for the rest of her life. A young doctor like Jim Rudd, for example.

Wednesday wept, but was completely incapable of fighting him for long. In the end, she made only one condition—that Dr. Rudd preserve the secrecy that Lorington had initiated. She didn't want to become a medical journal freak or a newspaper sob story.

The reasons why Fabian agreed had only a little to do with magnanimity. He wanted to have her oddities for himself alone. Sandra he had worn on his breast, like a flashing jewel hung from a pendant. Wednesday he would keep in a tiny chamois bag, examining her from time to time in a self-satisfied, miserly fashion.

And, after a while, he might have another, smaller jewel . . .

Jim Rudd accepted his conditions. And was astounded. "There is no navel at all!" he ejaculated when he had rejoined Fabian in his study, after the first examination. "I've palpated the skin for scar tissue, but there's not the slightest hint of it. And that's not the half of it! She has no discernible systole and diastole. Man, do you know what that means?"

"I'm not interested right now," Fabian told him. "Later, maybe. Do you think you can help her with these physical problems when they come up?"

"Oh, sure. At least as well as that old fellow."

"What about children? Can she have them?"

Rudd spread his hands. "I don't see why not. For all her peculiarities, she's a remarkably healthy young woman. And we have no reason to believe that this condition—whatever you want to call it—is hereditary. Of course, some part of it might be, in some strange way or other, but on the evidence . . ."

They were married, just before the start of Fabian's vacation, at City Hall. They came back to the office after lunch and told everyone about it. Fabian had already hired a new secretary to replace his wife.

Two months later, Fabian had managed to get her pregnant.

He was amazed at how upset she became, considering the meekness he had induced in her from the beginning of their marriage. He tried to be stern and to tell her he would have none of this nonsense, Dr. Rudd had said there was every reason to expect that she would have a normal baby, and that was that. But it didn't work. He tried gentle humor, cajolery. He even took her in his arms and told her he loved her too much not to want to have a little girl like her. But that didn't work either.

"Fabian, darling," she moaned "don't you understand? I'm not supposed to have a child. I'm not like other women."

He finally used something he had been saving as a last resort for this emergency. He took a book from the shelf and flipped it open. "I understand," he said. "It's half Dr. Lorington and his nineteenth-century superstitious twaddle, and half a silly little folk poem you read when you were a girl and that made a terrifying impression on you. Well, I can't do anything about Dr. Lorington at this point in your life, but I can do something about that poem. Here. Read this."

She read:

> Birthdays
>   by B. L. FARJEON
> Monday's child is fair of face,
> Tuesday's child is full of grace,
> Wednesday's child is loving and giving,
> Thursday's child works hard for a living,
> Friday's child is full of woe,
> Saturday's child has far to go,
> But the child that is born on the Sabbath-day
> Is brave and bonny, and good and gay.

Wednesday looked up and shook the tears from her eyes. "But I don't understand," she muttered in confusion. "That's not like the one I read."

He squatted beside her and explained patiently. "The one you read had two lines transposed, right? Wednes-

41

day's and Thursday's child had the lines that Friday's and Saturday's child have in this version and vice versa. Well, it's an old Devonshire poem originally, and no one knows for sure which version is right. I looked it up, especially for you. I just wanted to show you how silly you were, basing your entire attitude toward life on a couple of verses which could be read either way, not to mention the fact that they were written several centuries before anyone thought of naming you Wednesday."

She threw her arms around him and held on tightly. "Oh, Fabian, darling! Don't be angry with me. It's just that I'm so—*frightened!*"

Jim Rudd was a little concerned, too. "Oh, I'm pretty sure it will be all right, but I wish you'd waited until I had time to familiarize myself a bit more with the patient. The only thing, Fabe, I'll have to call in a first-rate obstetrician. I'd never dream of handling this myself. I can make him keep it quiet, about Wednesday and all that. But the moment she enters the delivery room, all bets are off. Too many odd things about her—they're bound to be noticed by some nurse, at least."

"Do the best you can," Fabian told him. "I don't want my wife involved in garish publicity, if it can be helped. But if it can't be—well, it's about time Wednesday learned to live in the real world."

The gestation period went along pretty well, with not much more than fairly usual complications. The obstetrical specialist Jim Rudd had suggested was as intrigued as anyone else by Wednesday's oddities, but he told them that the pregnancy was following a monotonously normal course and that the foetus seemed to be developing satisfactorily and completely on schedule.

Wednesday became fairly cheerful again. Outside of her minor fears, Fabian reflected, she was an eminently satisfactory and useful wife. She didn't exactly shine at parties where they mingled with other married couples from Slaughter, Stark and Slingsby, but she never committed a major faux pas either. She was, in fact, rather well liked, and, as she obeyed him faithfully in every particular, he had no cause at all for complaint.

42

He spent his days at the office handling the dry, minuscule details of paper work and personnel administration more efficiently than ever before, and his nights and weekends with a person he had every reason to believe was the most *different* woman on the face of the Earth. He was very well satisfied.

Near the end of her term, Wednesday did beg for permission to visit Dr. Lorington just once. Fabian had to refuse, regretfully but firmly.

"It's not that I mind his not sending us a congratulatory telegram or wedding gift, Wednesday. I really don't mind that at all. I'm not the kind of man to hold a grudge. But you're in good shape now. You're over most of your silly fears. Lorington would just make them come alive again."

And she continued to do what he said. Without argument, without complaint. She was really quite a good wife. Fabian looked forward to the baby eagerly.

One day, he received a telephone call at the office from the hospital. Wednesday had gone into labor while visiting the obstetrician. She'd been rushed to the hospital and given birth shortly after arrival to a baby girl. Both mother and child were doing well.

Fabian broke out the box of cigars he'd been saving for this occasion. He passed them around the office and received the felicitations of everybody up to and including Mr. Slaughter, Mr. Stark and both Mr. Slingsbys. Then he took off for the hospital.

From the moment he arrived in the Maternity Pavilion, he knew that something was wrong. It was the way people looked at him, then looked quickly away. He heard a nurse saying behind him: "That must be the father." His lips went tight and dry.

They took him in to see his wife. Wednesday lay on her side, her knees drawn up against her abdomen. She was breathing hard, but seemed to be unconscious. Something about her position made him feel acutely uncomfortable, but he couldn't decide exactly what it was.

"I thought this was going to be the natural childbirth method," he said. "She told me she didn't think you'd have to use anesthesia."

43

"We didn't use anesthesia," the obstetrician told him. "Now let's go to your child, Mr. Balik."

He let them fit a mask across his face and lead him to the glass-enclosed room where the new-born infants lay in their tiny beds. He moved slowly, unwillingly, a shrieking song of incomprehensible disaster building up slowly in his head.

A nurse picked a baby out of a bed that was off in a corner away from the others. As Fabian stumbled closer, he observed with a mad surge of relief that the child looked normal. There was no visible blemish or deformity. Wednesday's daughter would not be a freak.

But the infant stretched its arms out to him. "Oh, Fabian, darling," it lisped through toothless gums in a voice that was all too terrifyingly familiar. "Oh, Fabian, darling, the strangest, most unbelievable thing has happened!"

THE SERVANT PROBLEM

THIS *was the day of complete control* ...

Garomma, the Servant of All, the World's Drudge, the Slavey of Civilization, placed delicately scented fingertips to his face, closed his eyes and allowed himself to luxuriate in the sensation of ultimate power, absolute power, power such as no human being had even dared to dream of before this day.

Complete control. Complete ...

Except for one man. One single ambitious maverick of a man. One very *useful* man. Should he be strangled at his desk this afternoon, that was the question, or should he be allowed a few more days, a few more weeks, of heavily supervised usefulness? His treason, his plots, were unquestionably coming to a head. Well, Garomma would decide that later. At leisure.

Meanwhile, in all other respects, with everyone else, there was control. Control not only of men's minds but of their glands as well. And those of their children.

And, if Moddo's estimates were correct, of their children's children.

"Yea," Garomma muttered to himself, suddenly remembering a fragment of the oral text his peasant father had taught him years ago, "yea, unto the seventh generation."

What ancient book, burned in some long-ago educational fire, had that text come from, he wondered? His father would not be able to tell him, nor would any of his father's friends and neighbors; they had all been wiped out after the Sixth District Peasant Uprising thirty years ago.

An uprising of a type that could never possibly occur again. Not with complete control.

Someone touched his knee gently, and his mind ceased its aimless foraging. Moddo. The Servant of Education, seated below him in the depths of the vehicle, gestured obsequiously at the transparent, missile-proof cupola that surrounded his leader down to the waist.

"The people," he stated in his peculiar half-stammer. "There. Outside."

Yes. They were rolling through the gates of the Hovel of Service and into the city proper. On both sides of the street and far into the furthest distance were shrieking crowds as black and dense and exuberant as ants on a piece of gray earthworm. Garomma, the Servant of All, could not be too obviously busy with his own thoughts; he was about to be viewed by those he served so mightily.

He crossed his arms upon his chest and bowed to right and left in the little dome that rose like a tower from the squat black conveyance. Bow right, bow left, and do it humbly. Right, left—and humbly, humbly. Remember, you are the Servant of All.

As the shrieks rose in volume, he caught a glimpse of Moddo nodding approval from beneath. Good old Moddo. This was his day of triumph as well. The achievement of complete control was most thoroughly and peculiarly the achievement of the Servant of Education. Yet Moddo sat in heavy-shadowed anonymity behind the driver with Garomma's personal bodyguards; sat and tasted his triumph only with his leader's tongue—as he had for more than twenty-five years now.

Fortunately for Moddo, such a taste was rich enough for his system. Unfortunately, there were others—one other at least—who required more . . .

Garomma bowed to right and left and, as he bowed, looked curiously through the streaming webs of black-uniformed motorcycle police that surrounded his car. He looked at the people of Capital City, *his* people, his as everything and everyone on Earth was his. Jamming madly together on the sidewalks, they threw their arms wide as his car came abreast of them.

"Serve us, Garomma," they chanted. "Serve us! Serve us!"

He observed their contorted faces, the foam that appeared at the mouth-corners of many, the half-shut eyes and ecstatic expressions, the swaying men, the writhing women, the occasional individual who collapsed in an unnoticed climax of happiness. And he bowed. With his arms crossed upon his chest, he bowed. Right and left. Humbly.

Last week, when Moddo had requested his views on problems of ceremony and protocol relative to today's parade, the Servant of Education had commented smugly on the unusually high incidence of mob hysteria expected when his chief's face was seen. And Garomma had voiced a curiosity he'd been feeling for a long time.

"What goes on in their minds when they see me, Moddo? I know they worship and get exhilarated and all that. But what precisely do you fellows call the emotion when you talk about it in the labs and places such as the Education Center?"

The tall man slid his hand across his forehead in the gesture that long years had made thoroughly familiar to Garomma.

"They are experiencing a trigger release," he said slowly, staring over Garomma's shoulder as if he were working out the answer from the electronically pinpointed world map on the back wall. "All the tensions

46

these people accumulate in their daily round of niggling little prohibitions and steady coercions, all the frustrations of 'don't do this and don't do this, do *that*' have been organized by the Service of Education to be released explosively the moment they see your picture or hear your voice."

"Trigger release. Hm! I've never thought of it quite *that* way."

Moddo held up a hand in rigid earnestness. "After all, you're the one man whose life is supposedly spent in an abject obedience beyond anything they've ever known. The man who holds the—the intricate strands of the world's coordination in his patient, unwearying fingers; the ultimate and hardest-worked employee; the—the scapegoat of the multitudes!"

Garomma had grinned at Moddo's scholarly eloquence. Now, however, as he observed his screaming folk from under submissive eyelids, he decided that the Servant of Education had been completely right.

On the Great Seal of the World State was it not written: *All Men Must Serve Somebody, But Only Garomma Is the Servant of All"?*

Without him, they knew, and knew irrevocably, oceans would break through dikes and flood the land, infections would appear in men's bodies and grow rapidly into pestilences that could decimate whole districts, essential services would break down so that an entire city could die of thirst in a week, and local officials would oppress the people and engage in lunatic wars of massacre with each other. Without him, without Garomma working day and night to keep everything running smoothly, to keep the titanic forces of nature and civilization under control. They knew, because these things happened whenever "Garomma was tired of serving."

What were the unpleasant interludes of their lives to the implacable dreary—but, oh, so essential!—toil of his? Here, in this slight, serious-looking man bowing humbly right and left, right and left, was not only the divinity that made it possible for Man to exist comfortably on Earth, but also the crystallization of all the sub-races that ever enabled an exploited people to feel that things

47

could be worse, that relative to the societal muck beneath them, they were, in spite of their sufferings, as lords and monarchs in comparison.

No wonder they stretched their arms frantically to him, the Servant of All, the World's Drudge, the Slavey of Civilization, and screamed their triumphant demand with one breath, their fearful plea with the next: "Serve us, Garomma! Serve us, serve us, serve us!"

Didn't the docile sheep he had herded as a boy in the Sixth District mainland to the northwest, didn't the sheep also feel that he was their servant as he led them and drove them to better pastures and cooler streams, as he protected them from enemies and removed pebbles from their feet, all to the end that their smoking flesh would taste better on his father's table? But these so much more useful herds of two-legged, well-brained sheep were as thoroughly domesticated. And on the simple principle they'd absorbed that government was the servant of the people and the highest power in the government was the most abysmal servant.

His sheep. He smiled at them paternally, possessively, as his special vehicle rolled along the howling, face-filled mile between the Hovel of Service and the Educational Center. His sheep. And these policemen on motorcycles, these policemen on foot whose arms were locked against the straining crowds every step of the way, these were his sheepdogs. Another kind of domesticated animal.

That's all *he* had been, thirty-three years ago, when he'd landed on this island fresh from a rural Service of Security training school to take his first government job as a policeman in Capital City. A clumsy, over-excited sheep-dog. One of the least important sheep-dogs of the previous regime's Servant of All.

But three years later, the peasant revolt in his own district had given him his chance. With his special knowledge of the issues involved as well as the identity of the real leaders, he'd been able to play an important role in crushing the rebellion. And then, his new and important place in the Service of Security had enabled him to meet promising youngsters in the other services—Moddo, particularly, the first and most useful human he had personally domesticated.

With Moddo's excellent administrative mind at his disposal, he had become an expert at the gracious art of political throat-cutting, so that when his superior made his bid for the highest office in the world, Garomma had been in the best possible position to sell him out and become the new Servant of Security. And from that point, with Moddo puffing along in his wake and working out the minutiae of strategy, it had been a matter of a few years before he had been able to celebrate his own successful bid in the sizzling wreckage of the preceding administration's Hovel of Service.

But the lesson he had taught the occupants of that blasted, projectile-ridden place he had determined never to forget himself. He couldn't know how many Servants of Security before him had used their office to reach the mighty wooden stool of the Servant of All: after all, the history books, and all other books, were rewritten thoroughly at the beginning of every new regime; and the Oral Tradition, usually a good guide to the past if you could sift the facts out properly, was silent on this subject. It was obvious, however, that what he had done, another could do—that the Servant of Security was the logical, self-made heir to the Servant of All.

And the trouble was you couldn't do anything about the danger but be watchful.

He remembered when his father had called him away from childhood games and led him out to the hills to tend the sheep. How he had hated the lonesome, tiresome work! The old man had realized it and, for once, had softened sufficiently to attempt an explanation.

"You see, son, sheep are what they call domestic animals. So are dogs. Well, we can domesticate sheep and we can domesticate dogs to guard the sheep, but for a smart, wide-awake shepherd who'll know what to do when something real unusual comes up and will be able to tell us about it, well, for that we need a man."

"Gee, Pa," he had said, kicking disconsolately at the enormous shepherd's crook they'd given him, "then why don't you—whatdoyoucallit—*domesticate* a man?"

49

His father had chuckled and then started out heavily over the shaggy brow of the hill. "Well, there are people trying to do that, too, and they're getting better at it all the time. The only trouble, once you've got him domesticated, he isn't worth beans as a shepherd. He isn't sharp and excited once he's tamed. He isn't interested enough to be any use at all."

That was the problem in a nutshell, Garomma reflected. The Servant of Security, by the very nature of his duties, could not be a domesticated animal.

He had tried using sheep-dogs at the head of Security; over and over again he had tried them. But they were always inadequate and had to be replaced by men. And— one year, three years, five years in office—men sooner or later struck for supreme power and had to be regretfully destroyed.

As the current Servant of Security was about to be destroyed. The only trouble—the man was so damned useful! You had to time these things perfectly to get the maximum length of service from the rare, imaginative individual who filled the post to perfection and yet cut him down the moment the danger outweighed the value. And since, with the right man, the danger existed from the very start, you had to watch the scale carefully, unremittingly . . .

Garomma sighed. This problem was the only annoyance in a world that had been virtually machined to give him pleasure. But it was, inevitably, a problem that was with him always, even in his dreams. Last night had been positively awful.

Moddo touched his knee again to remind him that he was on exhibition. He shook himself and smiled his gratitude. One had to remember that dreams were only dreams.

They had the crowds behind them now. Ahead, the great metal gate of the Educational Center swung slowly open and his car rumbled inside. As the motorcycle policemen swung off their two-wheelers with a smart sidewise flourish, the armed guards of the Service of Education in their crisp white tunics came to attention.

Garomma, helped nervously by Moddo, clambered out of the car just as the Center Band, backed by the Center Choir, swung into the roaring, thrilling credo of *Humanity's Hymn:*

> *Garomma works day and night,*
> *Garomma's tasks are never light;*
> *Garomma lives in drudgery,*
> *For the sake of me, for the sake of thee . . ."*

After five verses, protocol having been satisfied, the band began *The Song of Education* and the Assistant Servant of Education, a poised, well-bred young man, came down the steps of the building. His arm-spread and "Serve us, Garomma," while perfunctory, was thoroughly correct. He stood to one side so that Garomma and Moddo could start up the steps and then swung in, straight-backed, behind them. The choirmaster held the song on a high, worshipping note.

They walked through the great archway with its carved motto, *All Must Learn from the Servant of All*, and down the great central corridor of the immense building. The gray rags that Garomma and Moddo wore flapped about them. The walls were lined with minor employees chanting, "Serve us, Garomma. Serve us! Serve us! Serve us!"

Not quite the insane fervor of the street mobs, Garomma reflected, but entirely satisfactory paroxysms nonetheless. He bowed and stole a glance at Moddo beside him. He barely restrained a smile. The Servant of Education looked as nervous, as uncertain as ever. Poor Moddo! He was just not meant for such a high position. He carried his tall, husky body with all the *élan* of a tired berry-picker. He looked like anything but the most important official in the establishment.

And that was one of the things that made him indispensable. Moddo was just bright enough to know his own inadequacy. Without Garomma, he'd still be checking statistical abstracts for interesting discrepancies in some minor department of the Service of Education. He *knew* he wasn't strong enough to stand by himself. Nor was he sufficiently outgoing to make useful alliances. And so Moddo, alone of all the Servants in the Cabinet, could be trusted completely.

In response to Moddo's diffident touch on his shoulder, he walked into the large room that had been so extravagantly prepared for him and climbed the little cloth-of-gold platform at one end. He sat down on the rough wooden stool at the top; a moment later, Moddo took the chair that was one step down, and the Assistant Servant of Education took the chair a further step below. The chief executives of the Educational Center, dressed in white tunics of the richest, most flowing cut, filed in slowly and stood before them. Garomma's personal bodyguards lined up in front of the platform.

And the ceremonies began. The ceremonies attendant upon complete control.

First, the oldest official in the Service of Education recited the appropriate passages from the Oral Tradition. How every year, in every regime, far back almost to prehistoric democratic times, a psychometric sampling had been taken of elementary school graduating classes all over the world to determine exactly how successful the children's political conditioning had been.

How every year there had been an overwhelming majority disclosed which believed the current ruler was the very pivot of human welfare, the mainspring of daily life, and a small minority—five per cent, seven per cent, three per cent—which had successfully resisted indoctrination and which, as adults, were to be carefully watched as potential sources of disaffection.

How with the ascension of Garomma and his Servant of Education, Moddo, twenty-five years ago, a new era of intensive mass-conditioning, based on much more ambitious goals, had begun.

The old man finished, bowed and moved back into the crowd. The Assistant Servant of Education rose and turned gracefully to face Garomma. He described these new goals which might be summed up in the phrase "complete control," as opposed to previous administrations' out-dated satisfaction with 97% or 95% control, and discussed the new extensive fear mechanisms and stepped-up psychometric spot-checks in the earlier grades—by which they were to be achieved. These techniques had all been worked out by Moddo—"under the never-failing inspiration and constant guidance of Garomma, the Servant of All"—and had, in a few years, resulted in a sampling which showed the number of independent juvenile minds to be less than one per cent. All others worshiped Garomma with every breath they took.

Thereafter, progress had been slower. They had absorbed the most brilliant children with the new conditioning process, but had hit the hard bedrock of the essential deviates, the psychological misfits whose personal maladjustments made it impossible for them to accept the prevailing attitudes of their social milieu, *whatever* these attitudes should happen to be. Over the years, techniques of conditioning had been painfully worked out which enabled even misfits to fit into society in the one respect of Garomma-worship and, over the years, the samplings indicated the negative doctrinal responses to be receding in the direction of zero: .016%, .007%, .0002%.

And *this* year. Well! The Assistant Servant of Education paused and took a deep breath. Five weeks ago, the Uniform Educational System of Earth had graduated a new crop of youngsters from the elementary schools. The customary planet-wide sampling had been taken on graduation day; collation and verification had just been completed. The results: negative response was zero to the very last decimal place! Control was complete.

Spontaneous applause broke out in the room, applause in which even Garomma joined. Then he leaned forward and placed his hand paternally, possessively on Moddo's head of unruly brown hair. At this unusual honor to their chief, the officials in the room cheered.

Under the noise, Garomma took the opportunity to ask Moddo, "What does the population in general know about this? What exactly are you telling them?"

Moddo turned his nervous, large-jawed face around. "Mostly just that it's a holiday. A lot of obscure stuff about you achieving complete control of the human environment all to the end of human betterment. Barely enough so that they can know it's something you like and can rejoice with you."

"In their own slavery. I like that." Garomma tasted the sweet flavor of unlimited rulership for a long moment. Then the taste went sour and he remembered. "Moddo, I want to take care of the Servant of Security matter this afternoon. We'll go over it as soon as we start back."

The Servant of Education nodded. "I have a few thoughts. It's not so simple, you know. There's the problem of the successor."

"Yes. There's always that. Well, maybe in a few more years, if we can sustain this sampling and spread the techniques to the maladjusted elements in the older adult population, we'll be able to start dispensing with Security altogether."

"Maybe. Strongly set attitudes are much harder to adjust, though. And you'll always need a security system in the top ranks of officialdom. But I'll do the best—I'll do the best I can."

Garomma nodded and sat back, satisfied. Moddo would always do his best. And on a purely routine level, that was pretty good. He raised a hand negligently. The cheering and the applause stopped. Another Education executive came forward to describe the sampling method in detail. The ceremony went on.

This was the day of complete control . . .

Moddo, the Servant of Education, the Ragged Teacher of Mankind, rubbed his aching forehead with huge, well-manicured fingers and allowed himself to luxuriate in the sensation of ultimate power, absolute power, power such as no human being had even dared to dream of before this day.

Complete control. Complete . . .

There was the one remaining problem of the successor to the Servant of Security. Garomma would want a decision from him as soon as they started back to the Hovel of Service; and he was nowhere near a decision. Either one of the two Assistant Servants of Security would be able to fill the job admirably, but that wasn't the question. The question was which one of the two men would be most likely to maintain at high pitch in Garomma the fears that Moddo had conditioned him to feel over a period of thirty years?

That, so far as Moddo was concerned, was the whole function of the Servant of Security; to serve as primary punching bag for the Servant of All's fear-ridden subconscious until such time as the mental conflicts reached a periodic crisis. Then, by removing the man around whom they had been trained to revolve, the pressure would be temporarily eased.

It was a little like fishing, Moddo decided. You fed the fish extra line by killing off the Servant of Security, and then you reeled it in quietly, steadily, in the next few years by surreptitiously dropping hints about the manifest ambitions of his successor. Only you never wanted to land the fish. You merely wanted to keep it hooked and constantly under your control.

The Servant of Education smiled an inch or two behind his face as he had trained himself to smile since early boyhood. Landing the fish? That would be the equivalent of becoming Servant of All himself. And what intelligent man could satisfy his lust for power with such an idiotic goal?

No, leave that to his colleagues, the ragged high officials in the Hovel of Service, forever scheming and plotting, making alliances and counter-alliances. The Servant of Industry, the Servant of Agriculture, the Servant of Science and the rest of those highly important fools.

To be the Servant of All meant being the target of plots, the very bull's eye of attention. An able man in this society must inevitably recognize that power—no matter how veiled or disguised—was the only valid aim in life. And the Servant of All—veiled and disguised though he might be in a hundred humbling ways—was power incarnate.

No. Far better to be known as the nervous, uncertain underling whose knees shook beneath the weight of responsibilities far beyond his abilities. Hadn't he heard their contemptuous voices behind his back?

". . . Garomma's administrative toy . . ."

". . . Garomma's fool of a spiritual valet . . ."

". . . nothing but a footstool, a very ubiquitous footstool, mind you, but a footstool nonetheless on which rests Garomma's mighty heel . . ."

". . . poor, colorless, jittery slob . . ."

". . . when Garomma sneezes, Moddo sniffles . . ."

But from that menial, despised position, to be the real source of all policy, the maker and breaker of men, the *de facto* dictator of the human race . . .

He brought his hand up once more and smoothed at his forehead. The headache was getting worse. And the official celebration of complete control was likely to take another hour yet. He should be able to steal away for twenty or thirty minutes with Loob the Healer, without getting Garomma too upset. The Servant of All had to be handled with special care at these crisis points. The jitters that had been induced in him were likely to become so overpowering that he might try to make a frantic decision for himself. And that possibility, while fantastically dim, must not be given a chance to develop. It was too dangerous.

For a moment, Moddo listened to the young man in front of them rattle on about modes and means, skew curves and correlation coefficients, all the statistical jargon that concealed the brilliance of the psychological revolution that he, Moddo, had wrought. Yes, they would be there another hour yet.

Thirty-five years ago, while doing his thesis in the Central Service of Education Post-Graduate Training School, he had found a magnificent nugget in the accumulated slag of several centuries of mass-conditioning statistics; the concept of *individual* application.

For a long while, he had found the concept incredibly difficult to close with: when all your training has been directed toward the efficient handling of human attitudes in terms of millions, the consideration of one man's attitudes and emotions is as slippery a proposition as an eel, freshly caught and moribundly energetic.

But after his thesis had been completed and accepted— the thesis on suggested techniques for the achievement of complete control which the previous administration had duly filed and forgotten—he had turned once more to the problem of individual conditioning.

And in the next few years, while working at his dull job in the Applied Statistics Bureau of the Service of Education, he had addressed himself to the task of refining the individual from the group, or reducing the major to the minor.

One thing became apparent. The younger your material, the easier your task—exactly as in mass-conditioning. But if you started with a child, it would be years before he would be able to operate effectively in the world on your behalf. And with a child you were faced with the constant counter-barrage of political conditioning which filled the early school years.

What was needed was a young man who already had a place of sorts in the government, but who, for some reason or other, had a good deal of unrealized—and *unconditioned*—potential. Preferably, also, somebody whose background had created a personality with fears and desires of a type which could serve as adequate steering handles.

Moddo began to work nights, going over the records of his office in search of that man. He had found two or three who looked good. That brilliant fellow in the Service of Transport, he reminisced, had seemed awfully interesting for a time. Then he had come across Garomma's papers.

And Garomma had been perfect. From the first. He was a directorial type, he was likable, he was clever—and he was very receptive.

"I could learn an awful lot from you," he had told Moddo shyly at their first meeting. "This is such a big, complicated place—Capital Island. So much going on all the time. I get confused just thinking about it. But you were born here. You really seem to know your way around all the swamps and bogs and snakepits."

Due to sloppy work on the part of the Sixth District Conditioning Commissioner, Garomma's home neighborhood had developed a surprising number of quasi-independent minds on all levels of intelligence. Most of them tended to revolution, especially after a decade of near-famine crops and exorbitant taxation. But Garomma had been ambitious; he had turned against his peasant background and entered the lower echelons of the Service of Security.

This meant that when the Sixth District Peasant Uprising occurred, his usefulness in its immediate suppression had earned him a much higher place. More important, it had given him freedom from the surveillance and extra adult conditioning which a man of his suspicious family associations might normally have expected.

It also meant that, once Moddo had maneuvered an introduction and created a friendship, he had at his disposal not only a rising star but a personality that was superb in its plasticity.

A personality upon which he could laboriously create the impress of his own image.

First, there had been that wonderful business of Garomma's guilt about disobeying his father that had eventually led to his leaving the farm altogether—and later to his becoming an informer against his own family and neighbors. This guilt, which had resulted in fear and therefore hatred for everything associated with its original objects, was easy to redirect to the person of his superior, the Servant of Security, and make that the new father-image.

Later, when Garomma had become Servant of All, he still retained—under Moddo's tireless ministrations—the same guilt and the same omnipresent fear of punishment toward whoever was the reigning Head of Security. Which was necessary if he was not to realize that his real master was the large man who sat at his right hand, constantly looking nervous and uncertain . . .

Then there had been education. And re-education. From the beginning, Moddo had realized the necessity of feeding Garomma's petty peasant arrogance and had abased himself before it. He gave the other man the impression that the subversive thoughts he was now acquiring were of his own creation, even leading him to believe that he was domesticating Moddo—curious how the fellow never escaped from his agricultural origins even in his metaphors!—instead of the other way around.

Because Moddo was now laying plans for a tremendous

future, and he didn't want them upset some day by the cumulative resentment one may develop toward a master and teacher; on the contrary, he wanted the plans reinforced by the affection one feels toward a pet dog whose nuzzling dependence constantly feeds the ego and creates a more ferocious counter-dependence than the owner ever suspects.

The shock that Garomma had exhibited when he began to realize that the Servant of All was actually the Dictator of All! Moddo almost smiled with his lips at the memory. Well, after all, when his own parents had suggested the idea years ago in the course of a private sailing trip they took together pursuant to his father's duties as a minor official in the Service of Fisheries and Marine—hadn't he been so upset that he'd let go of the tiller and vomited over the side? Losing your religion is a hard thing at any age, but it gets much harder as you get older.

On the other hand, Moddo had lost not only his religion at the age of six, but also his parents. They had done too much loose talking to too many people under the incorrect assumption that the then Servant of Security was going to be lax forever.

He rubbed his knuckles into the side of his head. This headache was one of the worst he'd had in days! He needed fifteen minutes at least—surely he could get away for fifteen minutes—with Loob. The Healer would set him up for the rest of the day, which, on all appearances, was going to be a tiring one. And he had to get away from Garomma, anyway, long enough to come to a clear-headed, personal decision on who was to be the next Servant of Security.

Moddo, the Servant of Education, the Ragged Teacher of Mankind, took advantage of a pause between speakers to lean back and say to Garomma: "I have a few administrative matters to check here before we start back. May I be excused? It—it won't take more than about twenty or twenty-five minutes."

Garomma scowled imperiously straight ahead. "Can't they wait? This is your day as much as mine. I'd like to have you near me."

"I know that, Garomma, and I'm grateful for the need.

But"—and now he touched the Servant of All's knee in supplication—"I beg of you to let me attend to them They are very pressing. One of them has to do—it has to do indirectly with the Servant of Security and may help you decide whether you want to dispense with him at this particular time."

Garomma's face immediately lost its bleakness. "In that case, by all means. But get back before the ceremony is over. I want us to leave together."

The tall man nodded and rose. He turned to face his leader. "Serve us, Garomma," he said with outstretched arms. "Serve us, serve us, serve us." He backed out of the room, always facing the Servant of All.

Out in the corridor, he strode rapidly through the saluting Center of Education guards and into his private elevator. He pressed the third-floor button. And then, as the door swept shut and the car began to rise, he permitted himself a single, gentle, mouth-curling smile.

The trouble he had taken to pound that one concept into Garomma's thick head: the basic principle in modern scientific government is to keep the government so unobtrusive as to appear non-existent, to use the illusion of freedom as a kind of lubricant for slipping on invisible shackles—above all, to rule in the name of anything but rulership!

Garomma himself had phrased it in his own laborious fashion one day when, shortly after their great coup, they stood together—both still uncomfortable in the rags of greatness—and watched the construction of the new Hovel of Service in the charred place where the old one had stood for almost half a century. A huge, colorful, revolving sign on top of the unfinished building told the populace that FROM HERE WILL YOUR EVERY WANT AND NEED BE ATTENDED TO, FROM HERE WILL YOU BE SERVED MORE EFFICIENTLY AND PLEASANTLY THAN EVER BEFORE. Garomma had stared at the sign which was being flashed on the video receivers of the world—in the homes as well as in factories, offices, schools and compulsory communal gatherings—every hour on the hour.

"It's like my father used to say," he told Moddo at last

with the peculiar heavy chuckle he used to identify a thought he felt was entirely original; "the right kind of salesman, if he talks long enough and hard enough, can convince a man that the thickest thorns feel as soft as roses. All he has to do is keep calling them roses, hey, Moddo?"

Moddo had nodded slowly, pretending to be overcome by the brilliance of the analysis and savoring its complexities for a few moments. Then, as always, merely appearing to be conducting an examination of the various latent possibilities in Garomma's ideas, he had proceeded to give the new Servant of All a further lesson.

He had underlined the necessity of avoiding all outward show of pomp and luxury, something the so-recently dead officials of the previous administration had tended to forget in the years before their fall. He had pointed out that Servants of Mankind must constantly appear to be just that—the humble instruments of the larger mass will. Then anyone who acted contrary to Garomma's whim would be punished, not for disobeying his ruler, but for acting against the overwhelming majority of the human race.

And he had suggested an innovation that had been in his mind for a long time; the occasional creation of disasters in regions that had been uninterruptedly loyal and obedient. This would accentuate the fact that the Servant of All was very human indeed, that his tasks were overwhelming and that he occasionally grew tired.

This would intensify the impression that the job of coordinating the world's goods and services had almost grown too complex to be handled successfully. It would spur the various Districts on to uncalled-for prodigies of frantic loyalty and self-regimentation, so that they at least would have the Servant of All's maximum attention.

"Of course," Garomma had agreed. "That's what I said. The whole point is not to let them know that you're running their lives and that they're helping you do it. You're getting the idea."

He was getting the idea! He, Moddo, who ever since his adolescence had been studying a concept that had originated centuries ago when mankind had begun to emerge from the primitive chaos of self-rule and personal

61

decision into the organized social universe of modern times . . . *he* was getting the idea!

He had smirked gratefully. But he had continued applying to Garomma himself the techniques that he was teaching Garomma to apply to the mass of men as a whole. Year in, year out, seemingly absorbed in the immensities of the project he had undertaken on behalf of the Service of Education, he had actually left its planning in the hands of subordinates while he concentrated on Garomma.

And today, while superficially acquiring complete control over the minds of an entire generation of human beings, he had tasted for the first time complete control over Garomma. For the past five years, he had been attempting to crystallize his ascendancy in a form that was simpler to use than complicated need-mechanisms and statement-patterns.

Today, for the first time, the weary hours of delicate, stealthy conditioning had begun to work out perfectly. The hand-signal, the touch-stimulus that he had organized Garomma's mind to respond to, had resulted in the desired responses every single time!

As he walked down the third-floor corridor to Loob's modest office, he searched for an adequate expression. It was like, he decided, being able to turn a whole vast liner by one touch on the wheel. The wheel activated the steering engine, the steering engine pushed against the enormous weight of rudder, and the rudder's movements eventually forced the great ship to swing about and change its course.

No, he reflected, let Garomma have his glorious moments and open adulation, his secret palaces and multitudes of concubines. He, Moddo, would settle for the single, occasional touch . . . and complete control.

The anteroom to Loob's office was empty. He stood there impatiently for a moment, then called out: "Loob! Isn't anyone taking care of this place? I'm in a hurry!"

A plump little man with a tiny pointed beard on his chin came scurrying out of the other room. "My secretary—everyone had to go downstairs when the Servant of All entered—things are so disrupted—she hasn't returned yet. But I was careful," he went on, catching up to his own breath, "to cancel all my appointments with other patients while you were in the building. Please come in."

Moddo stretched himself out on the couch in the Healer's office. "I can only spare about—about fifteen minutes. I have a very important decision to make, and I have a headache that's gouging out my—my·brains."

Loob's fingers circled Moddo's neck and began massaging the back of his head with a serene purposefulness. "I'll do what I can. Now try to relax. Relax. That's right. *Relax.* Doesn't this help?"

"A lot," Moddo sighed. He must find some way of working Loob into his personal entourage, to be with him whenever he had to travel with Garomma. The man was *invaluable.* It would be wonderful to have him always available in person. Just a matter of conditioning Garomma to the thought. And now *that* could be handled with the same suggestion. "Do you mind if I just talk?" he inquired. "I don't feel very much—very much like free association."

Loob sat down in the heavily upholstered chair behind the desk. "Do whatever you want. If you care to, go into what's troubling you at the moment. All we can hope to do in fifteen minutes is help you relax."

Moddo began to talk.

This was the day of complete control . . .
Loob, the Healer of Minds, the Assistant to the Third Assistant Servant of Education, threaded his fingers through the small, triangular beard that was his professional badge and allowed himself to luxuriate in the sensation of ultimate power, absolute power, power such as no human being had even dared to dream of before this day.

Complete control. Complete . . .

It would have been extremely satisfying to have handled the Servant of Security matter directly, but such pleasures would come in time. His technicians in the Bureau of Healing Research had almost solved the problem he had set them. Meanwhile he still had revenge and the enjoyment of unlimited dominion.

He listened to Moddo talking of his difficulties in a carefully guarded, non-specific fashion and held up a round fat hand to cover his grin. The man actually believed that after seven years of close therapeutic relationship, he could conceal such details from Loob!

But of course. He had to believe it. Loob had spent the first two years restructuring his entire psyche upon that belief, and then—and only then—had begun to effect transference on a total basis. While the emotions Moddo felt toward his parents in childhood were being duplicated relative to the Healer, Loob had begun to probe in the now unsuspicious mind. At first he hadn't believed what the evidence suggested. Then, as he got to know the patient much better he became completely convinced and almost breathless at the scope of his windfall.

For more than twenty-five years, Garomma, as the Servant of All, had ruled the human race, and for longer than that, Moddo, as a sort of glorified personal secretary, had controlled Garomma in every important respect.

So, for the past five years, he, Loob, as psychotherapist and indispensable crutch to an uncertain, broken ego, had guided Moddo and thus reigned over the world, undisputed, unchallenged—and thoroughly unsuspected.

The man behind the man behind the throne. What could be safer than that?

Of course, it would be more efficient to fasten his therapeutic grip directly on Garomma. But that would bring him out in the open far too much. Being the Servant of All's personal mental physician would make him the object of jealous scrutiny by every scheming high-echelon cabal.

No, it was better to be the one who had custody of the custodian, especially when the custodian appeared to be the most insignificant man in all the Hovel of Service officialdom.

And then, some day, when his technicians had come up with the answer he required, he might dispose of the Servant of Education and control Garomma at first-hand, with the new method.

He listened with amusement to Moddo discussing the Servant of Security matter in terms of a hypothetical individual in his own department who was about to be replaced. The question was which one of two extremely able subordinates should be given his job?

Loob wondered if the patient had any idea how transparent his subterfuges were. No, they rarely did. This was a man whose upset mind had been so manipulated that its continued sanity depended on two factors: the overpowering need to consult Loob whenever anything even mildly delicate came up, and the belief that he could be consulted without revealing the actual data of the situation.

When the voice on the couch had come to the end of its ragged, wandering summation, Loob took over. Smoothly, quietly, almost tonelessly, he reviewed what Moddo had said. On the surface he was merely restating the concepts of his patient in a more coherent way. Actually, he was reformulating them so that, considering his personal problems and basic attitudes, the Servant of Education would have no alternative. He would have to select the younger of the two candidates, the one whose background had included the least opposition to the Healers Guild.

Not that it made very much difference. The important thing was the proof of complete control. That was implicit in having made Moddo convince Garomma of the necessity of getting rid of a Servant of Security at a time when the Servant of All faced no particular mental crisis. When, in fact, his euphoria was at its height.

But there was, admittedly, the additional pleasure in finally destroying the man who, years ago as Chief of the Forty-seventh District's Security, had been responsible for the execution of Loob's only brother. The double achievement was as delicious as one of those two-flavor tarts for which the Healer's birthplace was famous. He sighed reminiscently.

Moddo sat up on the couch. He pressed his large, spreading hands into the fabric on either side and stretched. "You'd be amazed how much help this one short session has been, Loob. The—the headache's gone, the—the confusion's gone. Just talking about it seems to clarify everything. I know exactly what I have to do now."

"Good," drawled Loob the Healer in a gentle, carefully detached voice.

"I'll try to get back tomorrow for a full hour. And I've been thinking of having you transferred to my personal staff, so that you can straighten out—straighten out the kinks at the time they occur. I haven't reached a decision on it yet, though."

Loob shrugged and escorted his patient to the door. "That's entirely up to you. However you feel I can help you most."

He watched the tall, husky man walking down the corridor to the elevator. "*I haven't reached a decision on it yet, though.*" Well, he wouldn't—not until Loob did. Loob had put the idea into his mind six months ago, but had deferred having him take action on it. He wasn't sure that it would be a good idea to get even that close to the Servant of All as yet. And there was that wonderful little project in the Bureau of Healing Research which he still wanted to give maximum daily attention.

His secretary came in and went right to work at her typewriter. Loob decided to go downstairs and check on what had been done today. With all the fanfare attendant upon the Servant of All's arrival to celebrate complete control, the researchers' routine had no doubt been seriously interrupted. Still, the solution might come at any time. And he liked to examine their lines of investigation for potential fruitfulness: these technicians were blunderingly unimaginative!

As he walked down to the main floor, he wondered if Moddo, anywhere in the secret depths of his psyche, had any idea of how much he had come to depend on the Healer, how thoroughly he needed him. The fellow was such a tangle of anxiety and uncertainty—losing his parents as a child, the way he had, of course had not helped too much, but his many repressions had been in existence even then. He had never even remotely suspected that the reason he wanted Garomma to be the ostensible leader was because he was afraid of taking personal responsibility for anything. That the fake personality he was proud of presenting to the world was his real personality, the difference being that he had learned to use his fears and timidity in a positive fashion. But only up to a point. Seven years ago, when he had looked up Loob ("a fast bit of psychotherapy for some minor problems I've been having"), he'd been on the point of complete collapse. Loob had repaired the vast flapping structure on a temporary basis and given it slightly different functions. Functions for Loob.

He couldn't help wondering further if the ancients would have been able to do anything basic for Moddo. The ancients, according to the Oral Tradition at least, had developed, just before the beginning of the modern era, a psychotherapy that accomplished wonders of change and personal reorganization for the individual.

But to what end? No serious attempt to use the method for its obvious purpose, for the only purpose of any method . . . *power*. Loob shook his head. Those ancients had been so incredibly naive! And so much of their useful knowledge had been lost. Concepts like super-ego merely existed in the Oral Tradition of the Healers Guild as words; there was no clue as to their original meaning. They might be very useful today, properly applied.

On the other hand, were most of the members of his own modern Healers Guild across the wide sea, any less naive, including his father and the uncle who was now its reigning head? From the day when he had passed the Guild's final examinations and begun to grow the triangular beard of master status, Loob had seen that the ambitions of his fellow-members were ridiculously limited. Here, in this very city, where, according to legend, the Guild of the Healers of Minds had originated, each member asked no more of life than to use his laboriously learned skill at transference to acquire power over the lives of ten or fifteen wealthy patients.

Loob had laughed at these sparse objectives. He had seen the obvious goal which his colleagues had been overlooking for years. The more powerful the individual whom you subjected to transference and in whom you created a complete dependence the more power you, as his healer, enjoyed. The world's power center was on Capital Island across the great ocean to the east. And it was there that Loob determined to go.

It hadn't been easy. The strict rules of custom against changing your residence except on official business had stood in his way for a decade. But once the wife of the Forty-seventh District's Communications Commissioner had become his patient, it got easier. When the commissioner had been called to Capital Island for promotion to the Second Assistant Servantship of Communication, Loob had gone with the family; he was now indispensable. Through them he had secured a minor job in the Service of Education. Through that job, practicing his profession on the side, he had achieved enough notice to come to the august attention of the Servant of Education himself.

He hadn't really expected to go this far. But a little luck, a great deal of skill and constant, unwinking alertness had made an irresistible combination. Forty-five minutes after Moddo had first stretched out on his couch, Loob had realized that he, with all of his smallness and plumpness and lack of distinction, was destined to rule the world.

Now the only question was what to do with that rule. With wealth and power unlimited.

Well, for one thing there was his little research project. That was very interesting, and it would serve, once it came to fruition, chiefly to consolidate and insure his power. There were dozens of little pleasures and properties that were now his, but their enjoyment tended to wear off with their acquisition. And finally there was knowledge.

Knowledge. Especially forbidden knowledge. He could now enjoy it with impunity. He could collate the various Oral Traditions into one intelligible whole and be the only man in the world who knew what had really happened in the past. He had already discovered, through the several teams of workers he had set at the task, such tidbits as the original name of his birthplace, lost years ago in a numbering system that had been created to destroy patriotic associations inimical to the world state. Long before it had been the Fifth City of the Forty-seventh

District, he had learned, it had been Austria, the glorious capital of the proud Viennese Empire. And this island on which he stood had been Havanacuba, no doubt once a great empire in its own right which had established hegemony over all other empires somewhere in the dim warfilled beginnings of modern times.

Well, these were highly personal satisfactions. He doubted very much if Garomma, for example, would be interested to know that he hailed, not from the Twentieth Agricultural Region of the Sixth District, but from a place called Canada, one of the forty-eight constituent republics of the ancient Northern United States of America. But he, Loob, was interested. Every additional bit of knowledge gave you additional power over your fellowmen, that some day, some way, would be usable.

Why, if Moddo had had any real knowledge of the transference techniques taught in the upper lodges of the Guild of the Healers of Minds, he might still be running the world himself! But no. It was inevitable that a Garomma should actually be no more than a creature, a thing, of Moddo. It was inevitable that a Moddo, given the peculiar forces that had informed him, should inexorably have had to come to Loob and pass under his control. It was also inevitable that Loob, with his specialized knowledge of what could be done with the human mind, should be the only independent man on Earth today. It was also very pleasant.

He wriggled a little bit, very satisfied with himself, gave his beard a final finger-comb, and pushed into the Bureau of Healing Research.

The chief of the bureau came up rapidly and bowed. "Nothing new to report today." He gestured at the tiny cubicles in which the technicians sat at old books or performed experiments on animals and criminally convicted humans. "It took them a while to get back to work, after the Servant of All arrived. Everyone was ordered out into the main corridor for regulation empathizing with Garomma."

"I know," Loob told him. "I don't expect much progress on a day like this. Just so you keep them at it. It's a big problem."

The other man shrugged enormously. "A problem which, as far as we can tell, has never been solved before. The ancient manuscripts we've discovered are all in terrible shape, of course. But those that mention hypnotism all agree that it can't occur under any of the three conditions you want: against the individual's will, contrary to his personal desires and best judgment, and maintaining him over a long period of time in the original state of subjection without need for new applications. I'm not saying it's impossible, but—"

"But it's very difficult. Well, you've had three and a half years to work on it, and you'll have as much more time as you need. *And* equipment. *And* personnel. Just ask. Meanwhile, I'll wander around and see how your men are doing. You needn't come with me. I like to ask my own questions."

The bureau chief bowed again and turned back to his desk in the rear of the room. Loob, the Healer of Minds, the Assistant to the Third Assistant Servant of Education, walked slowly from cubicle to cubicle, watching the work, asking questions, but mostly noting the personal quality of the psychological technician in each cubicle.

He was convinced that the right man could solve the problem. And it was just a matter of finding the right man and giving him maximum facilities. The right man would be clever enough and persistent enough to follow up the right lines of research, but too unimaginative to be appalled by a goal which had eluded the best minds for ages.

And once the problem was solved—then in one short interview with Garomma, he could place the Servant of All under his direct, personal control for the rest of his life and dispense with the complications of long therapeutic sessions with Moddo where he constantly had to suggest, and suggest in roundabout fashion, rather than give simple, clear and unambiguous orders. Once the problem was solved—

He came to the last cubicle. The pimply-faced young man who sat at the plain brown table studying a ripped and damp-rotted volume didn't hear him come in. Loob studied him for a moment.

What frustrated, bleak lives these young technicians
70

must lead! You could see it in the tightly set lines of their all-too-similar faces. Growing up in one of the most rigidly organized versions of the world state that a ruler had yet contrived, they didn't have a thought that was in any way their own, could not dream of tasting a joy that had not been officially allotted to them.

And yet this fellow was the brightest of the lot. If any one in the Bureau of Healing Research could develop the kind of perfect hypnotic technique Loob required, he could. Loob had been watching him with growing hope for a long time now.

"How is it coming, Sidothi?" he asked.

Sidothi looked up from his book.

"Shut the door," he said.

Loob shut the door.

This was the day of complete control ...

Sidothi, the Laboratory Assistant, Psychological Technician Fifth Class, snapped his fingers in Loob's face and allowed himself to luxuriate in the sensation of ultimate power, absolute power, power such as no human being had even dared to dream of before this day.

Complete control. Complete ...

Still sitting, he snapped his fingers again.

He said: "Report."

The familiar glazed look came into Loob's eyes. His body stiffened. His arms hung limply at his sides. In a steady, toneless voice he began to deliver his report.

Magnificent. The Servant of Security would be dead in a few hours and the man Sidothi liked would take his place. For an experiment in complete control, it had worked out to perfection. That was all it had been; an attempt to find out if—by creating a feeling of vengefulness in Loob for the sake of a non-existent brother—he could force the Healer to act on a level he always wanted to avoid; making Moddo do something that the Servant of Education had no interest at all in doing. That was to prod Garomma into an action against the Servant of Security at a time when Garomma was in no particular mental crisis.

The experiment had worked perfectly. He'd pushed a

little domino named Loob three days ago, and a whole series of other little dominoes had begun to fall one right after the other. Today, when the Servant of Security was strangled at his desk, the last one would have fallen.

Yes, control was absolutely complete.

Of course, there had been another, minor reason why he had elected to conduct this experiment in terms of the Servant of Security's life. He didn't like the man. He'd seen him drink a liqueur in public four years ago. Sidothi didn't believe the Servants of Mankind should do such things. They should lead clean simple, abstemious lives; they should be an example to the rest of the human race.

He'd never seen the Assistant Servant of Security whom he had ordered Loob to have promoted, but he had heard that the fellow lived very narrowly, without luxury even in private. Sidothi liked that. That was the way it should be.

Loob came to the end of his report and stood waiting. Sidothi wondered whether he should order him to give up this bad, boastful idea of controlling Garomma directly. No, that wouldn't do: that attitude led into the mechanism of coming down to the Bureau of Healing Research every day to check on progress. While a simple order to come in daily would suffice, still Sidothi felt that until he had examined all aspects of his power and become thoroughly familiar with its use, it was wise to leave original personality mechanisms in place, so long as they didn't get in the way of anything important.

And that reminded him. There *was* an interest of Loob's which was sheer time-wasting. Now, when he was certain of absolute control, was a good time to get rid of it.

"You will drop this research into historical facts," he ordered. "You will use the time thus freed for further detailed examination of Moddo's psychic weaknesses. And you will find that more interesting than studying the past. That is all."

He snapped his fingers in Loob's face, waited a moment, then snapped them again. The Healer of Minds took a deep breath, straightened and smiled.

"Well, keep at it," he said, encouragingly.

"Thank you, sir. I will," Sidothi assured him.

Loob opened the door of the cubicle and walked out, pompously, serenely. Sidothi stared after him. The idiotic assurance of the man—that once the process of complete control by hypnotic technique was discovered it would be given to Loob!

Sidothi had begun to reach the answer three years ago. He had immediately covered up, letting his work take a superficially different line. Then, when he had the technique perfected, he'd used it on Loob himself. Naturally.

At first he'd been shocked, almost sickened, when he found out how Loob controlled Moddo, how Moddo controlled Garomma, the Servant of All. But after a while, he'd adjusted to the situation well enough. After all, ever since the primary grades, the only reality he and his contemporaries had accepted completely was the reality of power. Power in each class, in each club, in each and every gathering of human beings, was the only thing worth fighting for. And you chose an occupation not only because you were most fitted for it, but because it gave the greatest promise of power to a person of your particular interests and aptitude.

But he'd never dreamed of, never imagined, this much power! Well, he had it. That was reality, and reality was to be respected above all else. Now the problem was what to do with his power.

And that was a very hard question to answer. But the answer would come in time. Meanwhile, there was the wonderful chance to make certain that everyone did his job right, that bad people were punished. He intended to stay in his menial job until the proper time came for promotion. There was no need at the moment to have a big title. If Garomma could rule as the Servant of All, he could rule Garomma at third or fourth hand as a simple Psychological Technician Fifth Class.

But in what way exactly did he want to rule Garomma? What important things did he want to make Garomma do?

A bell rang. A voice called out of a loudspeaker set high in the wall. "Attention! Attention, all personnel! The Servant of All will be leaving the Center in a few minutes.

73

Everyone to the main corridor to beg for his continued service to mankind. Everyone—"

Sidothi joined the mob of technicians pouring out of the huge laboratory room. People were coming out of offices on both sides of them. He was swept up with a crowd constantly enlarging from the elevators and stairways to the main corridor where the Service of Education guards prodded them and jammed them against the walls.

He smiled. If they only knew whom they were pushing! Their ruler, who could have any one of them executed. The only man in the world who could do anything he wanted to do. *Anything.*

There was sudden swirling movement and a cheer at the far distant end of the corridor. Everyone began to shuffle about nervously, everyone tried to stand on tip-toe in order to see better. Even the guards began to breathe faster.

The Servant of All was coming.

The cries grew more numerous, more loud. People in front of them were heaving about madly. And suddenly Sidothi saw him!

His arms went up and out in a flashing paroxysm of muscles. Something tremendous and delighted seemed to press on his chest and his voice screamed, "Serve us, Garomma! Serve us! Serve us! Serve us!" He was suffused with heaving waves of love, love such as he never knew anywhere else, love for Garomma, love for Garomma's parents, love for Garomma's children, love for anything and everything connected with Garomma. His body writhed, almost without coordination, delicious flames licked up his thighs and out from his armpits, he twisted and turned, danced and hopped, his very stomach seeming to strain against his diaphragm in an attempt to express its devotion. None of which was very strange, considering that these phenomena had been conditioned in him since early childhood . . .

"Serve us, Garomma!" he shrieked, bubbles of saliva growing out of the corner of his mouth. "Serve us! Serve us! Serve us!"

He fell forward, between two guards, and his outstretched fingertips touched a rustling flapping rag just as the Servant of All strode by. His mind abruptly roared off into the furthest, most hidden places of ecstasy. He fainted, still babbling. "*Serve* us, O Garomma."

When it was all over, his fellow-technicians helped him back to the Bureau of Healing Research. They looked at him with awe. It wasn't every day you managed to touch one of Garomma's rags. What it must do to a person!

It took Sidothi almost half an hour to recover.

THIS WAS THE DAY OF COMPLETE CONTROL.

PARTY OF THE TWO PARTS

GALACTOGRAM FROM STELLAR SERGEANT O-DIK-VEH, COMMANDER OF OUTLYING PATROL OFFICE 1001625, TO HEADQUARTERS DESK SERGEANT HOY-VEH-CHALT, GALACTIC PATROL HEADQUARTERS ON VEGA XXI—(PLEASE NOTE: THIS IS TO BE TRANSMITTED AS A PERSONAL, NOT OFFICIAL, MESSAGE AND AS SUCH WILL BE CHARGED USUAL HYPERSPACE RATES)

MY DEAR HOY:

I am deeply sorry to trouble you again, but, Hoy, am I in a jam! Once more, it's not something that I did wrong, but something I didn't do right—what the Old One is sure to wheeze is "a patent dereliction of obvious duty." And since I'm positive he'll be just as confused as I, once the prisoners I'm sending on by slow light-transport arrive (when he reads the official report that I drew up and am transmitting with them, I can see him dropping an even dozen of his jaws), I can only hope that this advance message will give you enough time to consult the best legal minds in Vegan Headquarters and get some sort of solution worked out.

If there's any kind of solution available by the time he

reads my report, the Old One won't be nearly as angry at my dumping the problem on his lap. But I have an uneasy, persistent fear that Headquarters is going to get as snarled up in this one as my own office. If it does, the Old One is likely to remember what happened in Outlying Patrol Office 1001625 the last time—and then, Hoy, you will be short one spore-cousin.

It's a dirty business all around, a real dirty business. I use the phrase advisedly. In the sense of *obscene*, if you follow me.

As you've no doubt suspected by now, most of the trouble has to do with that damp and irritating third planet of Sol, the one that many of its inhabitants call Earth. Those damned chittering bipeds cause me more sleeplessness than any other species in my sector. Sufficiently advanced technologically to be almost at Stage 15 —self-developed interplanetary travel—they are still centuries away from the usually concurrent Stage 15A— friendly contact by the galactic civilization.

They are, therefore, still in Secretly Supervised Status, which means that I have to maintain a staff of about two hundred agents on their planet, all encased in clumsy and uncomfortable protoplasmic disguises, to prevent them from blowing their silly selves up before the arrival of their spiritual millennium.

On top of everything, their solar system only has nine planets, which means that my permanent headquarters office can't get any farther away from Sol than the planet they call Pluto, a world whose winters are bearable, but whose summers are unspeakably hot. I tell you, Hoy, the life of a stellar sergeant isn't all *gloor* and *skubbets,* no matter what Rear Echelon says.

In all honesty, though, I should admit that the difficulty did not originate on Sol III this time. Ever since their unexpected and uncalled-for development of nuclear fission, which as you know, cost me a promotion, I've doubled the number of undercover operatives on the planet and given them stern warning to report the slightest technological spurt immediately. I doubt that these humans could invent so much as an elementary time-machine now, without my knowing of it well in advance.

No, this time it all started on Rugh VI, the world known to those who live on it as Gtet. If you consult your atlas, Hoy, you'll find Rugh is a fair-sized yellow dwarf star on the outskirts of the Galaxy, and Gtet an extremely insignificant planet which has only recently achieved the status of Stage 19—primary interstellar citizenship.

The Gtetans are a modified ameboid race who manufacture a fair brand of *ashkebac*, which they export to their neighbors on Rugh IX and XII. They are a highly individualistic people and still experience many frictions living in a centralized society. Despite several centuries of advanced civilization, most Gtetans look upon the Law as a delightful problem in circumvention rather than as a way of life.

An ideal combination with my bipeds of Earth, eh?

It seems that a certain L'payr was one of the worst troublemakers on Gtet. He had committed almost every crime and broken almost every law. On a planet where fully one-fourth of the population is regularly undergoing penal rehabilitation, L'payr was still considered something quite special. A current Gtetan saying, I understand, puts it, "You're like L'payr, fellow—you don't know *when* to stop!"

Nonetheless, L'payr had reached the point where it was highly important that he did stop. He had been arrested and convicted for a total of 2,342 felonies, just one short of the 2,343 felonies which, on Gtet, make one a habitual criminal and, therefore, subject to life imprisonment. He made a valiant effort to retire from public life and devote himself to contemplation and good works but it was too late. Almost against his will, as he insisted to me under examination in my office, he found his mind turning to foul deeds left undone, illegalities as yet unperpetrated.

And so one day, quite casually—hardly noticing, as it were—he committed another major crime. But this one was so ineffably ugly, involving an offense against the moral code as well as civil legislation, that the entire community turned against L'payr.

He was caught selling pornography to juvenile Gtetans.

The indulgence that a celebrity may enjoy turned to

wrath and utter contempt. Even the Gtetan Protective Association of Two Thousand Time Losers refused to raise funds for his bail. As his trial approached, it became obvious to L'payr that he was in for it. His only hope lay in flight.

He pulled the most spectacular coup of his career—he broke out of the hermetically sealed vault in which he was being guarded around the clock (how he did this, he consistently refused to tell me up to the time of his lamented demise or whatever you want to call it) and escaped to the spaceport near the prison. There, he managed to steal aboard the pride of the Gtetan merchant fleet, a newly developed interstellar ship equipped with two-throttle hyperspace drive.

This ship was empty, waiting for a crew to take it out on its maiden run.

Somehow, in the few hours at his disposal before his escape was known, L'payr figured out the controls of the craft and managed to lift it off Gtet and into hyperspace. He had no idea at this time that, since the ship was an experimental model, it was equipped with a transmitting device that kept the spaceport informed of its location.

Thus, though they lacked the facilities to pursue him, the Gtetan police always knew exactly where he was. A few hundred ameboid vigilantes did start after him in old-fashioned, normal-drive ships, but after a month or so of long and fatiguing interstellar travel at one-hundredth his speed, they gave up and returned home.

For his hideout, L'payr wanted a primitive and unimportant corner of the Galaxy. The region around Sol was ideal. He materialized out of hyperspace about halfway between the third and fourth planets. But he did it very clumsily (after all, Hoy, the best minds of his race are just beginning to understand the two-throttle drive) and lost all of his fuel in the process. He barely managed to reach Earth and come down.

The landing was effected at night and with all drives closed, so that no one on the planet saw it. Because living conditions on Earth are so different from Gtet, L'payr knew that his mobility would be very limited. His one hope was to get help from the inhabitants. He had to pick a spot where possible contacts would be at maximum and yet accidental discovery of his ship would be at minimum. He chose an empty lot in the suburbs of Chicago and quickly dug his ship in.

Meanwhile, the Gtetan police communicated with me as the local commanding officer of the Galactic Patrol. They told me where L'payr was hidden and demanded extradition. I pointed out that, as yet, I lacked jurisdiction, since no crime of an *interstellar* nature had been committed. The stealing of the ship had been done on his home planet—it had not occurred in deep space. If, however, he broke any galactic law while he was on Earth, committed any breach of the peace, no matter how slight . . .

"How about that?" the Gtetan police asked me over the interstellar radio. "Earth is on Secretly Supervised Status, as we understand it. It is illegal to expose it to superior civilizations. Isn't L'payr landing there in a two-throttle hyperspace-drive ship enough of a misdemeanor to entitle you to pick him up?"

"Not by itself," I replied. "The ship would have to be seen and understood for what it was by a resident of the planet. From what we here can tell, no such observation was made. And so long as he stays in hiding, doesn't tell any human about us and refrains from adding to the technological momentum of Earth, L'payr's galactic citizenship has to be respected. I have no legal basis for an arrest."

Well, the Gtetans grumbled about what were they paying the star tax for, anyway, but they saw my point. They warned me, though, about L'payr—sooner or later his criminal impulses would assert themselves. He was in an impossible position, they insisted. In order to get the fuel necessary to leave Earth before his supplies ran out, he'd have to commit some felony or other—and as soon as he did so and was arrested, they wanted their extradition request honored.

"The filthy, evil-minded old pervert," I heard the police chief mutter as he clicked off.

I don't have to tell you how I felt, Hoy. A brilliant, imaginative ameboid criminal at large on a planet as volatile culturally as Earth! I notified all our agents in North

America to be on the alert and settled back to wait it out with prayerfully knotted tentacles.

L'payr had listened to most of this conversation over his own ship's receiver. Naturally, the first thing he did was to remove the directional device which had enabled the Gtetan police to locate him. Then, as soon as it was dark again, he managed, with what must have been enormous difficulty, to transport himself and his little ship to another area of the city. He did this, too, without being observed.

He made his base in a slum tenement neighborhood that had been condemned to make way for a new housing project and therefore was practically untenanted. Then he settled back to consider his problem.

Because, Hoy, he had a problem.

He didn't want to get in any trouble with the Patrol, but if he didn't get his pseudopods on a substantial amount of fuel very soon, he'd be a dead ameboid. Not only did he need the fuel to get off Earth, but the converters—which, on this rather primitive Gtetan vessel, changed waste matter back into usable air and food—would be stopping very soon if they weren't stoked up, too.

His time was limited, his resources almost non-existent. The spacesuits with which the ship was furnished, while cleverly enough constructed and able to satisfy the peculiar requirements of an entity of constantly fluctuating format, had not been designed for so primitive a planet as Earth. They would not operate too effectively for long periods away from the ship.

He knew that my OP office had been apprised of his landing and that we were just waiting for some infraction of even the most obscure minor law. Then we'd pounce— and, after the usual diplomatic formalities, he'd be on his way back to Gtet, for a nine-throttle Patrol ship could catch him easily. It was obvious that he couldn't do as he had originally planned—make a fast raid on some human supply center and collect whatever stuff he needed.

His hope was to make a trade. He'd have to find a human with whom he could deal and offer something that, to this particular human in any case, was worth the quantity of fuel L'payr's ship needed to take him to a less policed corner of the Cosmos. But almost everything on the ship was essential to its functioning. And L'payr had to make his trade without (1) giving away the existence and nature of the galactic civilization, or (2) providing the inhabitants of Earth with any technological stimulus.

L'payr later said that he thought about the problem until his nucleus was a mass of corrugations. He went over the ship, stem to stern, again and again, but everything a human might consider acceptable was either too useful or too revealing. And then, just as he was about to give up, he found it.

The materials he needed were those with which he had committed his last crime!

According to Gtetan law, you see, Hoy, all evidence pertaining to a given felony is retained by the accused until the time of his trial. There are very complicated reasons for this, among them the Gtetan juridical concept that every prisoner is *known* to be guilty until he manages, with the aid of lies, loopholes and brilliant legalisms, to convince a hard-boiled and cynical jury of his peers that they should, in spite of their knowledge to the contrary, declare him innocent. Since the burden of the proof rests with the prisoner, the evidence does likewise. And L'payr, examining this evidence, decided that he was in business.

What he needed now was a customer. Not only someone who wanted to buy what he had to sell, but a customer who had available the fuel he needed. And in the neighborhood which was now his base of operations, customers of this sort were rare.

Being Stage 19, the Gtetans are capable of the more primitive forms of telepathy—only at extremely short ranges, of course, and for relatively brief periods of time. So, aware that my secret agents had already begun to look for him and that, when they found him, his freedom of action would be even more circumscribed, L'payr desperately began to comb through the minds of any terrestrials within three blocks of his hideout.

Days went by. He scuttled from mind to mind like an

insect looking for a hole in a collector's jar. He was forced to shut the ship's converter down to one-half operation, then to one-third. Since this cut his supply of food correspondingly, he began to hunger. For lack of activity, his contractile vacuole dwindled to the size of pinpoint. Even his endoplasm lost the turgidity of the healthy ameboid and became dangerously thin and transparent.

And then one night, when he had about determined to take his chances and steal the fuel he needed, his thoughts ricocheted off the brain of a passerby, came back unbelievingly, examined further and were ecstatically convinced. A human who not only could supply his needs, but also, and more important, might be in the market for Gtetan pornography!

In other words, Mr. Osborne Blatch.

This elderly teacher of adolescent terrestrials insisted throughout all my interrogations that, to the best of his knowledge, no mental force was used upon him. It seems that he lived in a new apartment house on the other side of the torn-down tenement area and customarily walked in a wide arc around the rubble because of the large number of inferior and belligerent human types which infested the district. On this particular night, a teachers' meeting at his high school having detained him, he was late for supper and decided, as he had once or twice before, to take a short cut. He claims that the decision to take a short cut was his own.

Osborne Blatch says that he was striding along jauntily, making believe his umbrella was a malacca cane, when he seemed to hear a voice. He says that, even at first hearing, he used the word "seemed" to himself because, while the voice definitely had inflection and tone, it was somehow completely devoid of volume.

The voice said, "Hey, bud! C'mere!"

He turned around curiously and surveyed the rubble to his right. All that was left of the building that had once been there was the lower half of the front entrance. Since everything else around it was completely flat, he saw no place where a man could be standing.

But as he looked, he heard the voice again. It sounded

82

greasily conspiratorial and slightly impatient. "C'mere, bud. *C'mere!*"

"What—er—what *is* it, sir?" he asked in a cautiously well-bred way, moving closer and peering in the direction of the voice. The bright street light behind him, he said, improved his courage as did the solid quality of the very heavy old-fashioned umbrella he was carrying.

"C'mere. I got somp'n to show you. C'mon!"

Stepping carefully over loose brick and ancient garbage, Mr. Blatch came to a small hollow at one side of the ruined entrance. And filling it was L'payr or, as he seemed at first glance to the human, a small, splashy puddle of purple liquid.

I ought to point out now, Hoy—and the affidavits I'm sending along will substantiate it—that at no time did Mr. Blatch recognize the viscous garment for a spacesuit, nor did he ever see the Gtetan ship which L'payr had hidden in the rubble behind him in its completely tenuous hyperspatial state.

Though the man, having a good imagination and a resilient mind, immediately realized that the creature before him must be extraterrestrial, he lacked overt technological evidence to this effect, as well as to the nature and existence of our specific galactic civilization. Thus, here at least, there was no punishable violation of Interstellar Statute 2,607,193, Amendments 126 through 509.

"What do you have to show me?" Mr. Blatch asked courteously, staring down at the purple puddle. "And where, may I ask, are you from? Mars? Venus?"

"Listen, bud, y'know what's good for ya, y'don't ast such questions. Look, I got somep'n for ya. Hot stuff. *Real* hot!"

Mr. Blatch's mind, no longer fearful of having its owner assaulted and robbed by the neighborhood tough it had originally visualized, spun off to a relevant memory, years old, of a trip abroad. There had been that alley in Paris and the ratty little Frenchman in a torn sweater . . .

"What would that be?" he asked.

A pause now, while L'payr absorbed new impressions. "Ah-h-h," said the voice from the puddle. "I 'ave somezing to show M'sieu zat M'sieu weel like vairry much. If M'sieu weel come a little closair?"

M'sieu, we are to understand, came a leetle closair. Then the puddle heaved up in the middle, reaching out a pseudopod that held flat, square objects, and telepathed hoarsely, " 'Ere, M'sieu. Feelthy peekshures."

Although taken more than a little aback, Blatch merely raised both eyebrows interrogatively and said, "Ah? Well, well!"

He shifted the umbrella to his left hand and, taking the pictures as they were given to him, one at a time, examined each a few steps away from L'payr, where the light of the street lamp was stronger.

When all the evidence arrives, you will be able to see for yourself, Hoy, what they were like. Cheap prints, calculated to excite the grossest ameboid passions. The Gtetans, as you may have heard, reproduce by simple asexual fission, but only in the presence of saline solution —sodium chloride is comparatively rare on their world.

The first photograph showed a naked ameba, fat and replete with food vacuoles, splashing lazily and formlessly at the bottom of a metal tank in the completely relaxed state that precedes reproducing.

The second was like the first, except that a trickle of salt water had begun down one side of the tank and a few pseudopods had lifted toward it inquiringly. To leave nothing to the imagination, a sketch of the sodium chloride molecule had been superimposed on the upper right corner of the photograph.

In the third picture, the Gtetan was ecstatically awash in the saline solution, its body distended to maximum, dozens of pseudopods thrust out, throbbing. Most of the chromatin had become concentrated in chromosomes about the equator of the nucleus. To an ameba, this was easily the most exciting photograph in the collection.

The fourth showed the nucleus becoming indented between the two sets of sibling chromosomes—while, in the fifth, with the division completed and the two nuclei at opposite ends of the reproducing individual, the entire cytoplasmic body had begun to undergo constriction about its middle. In the sixth, the two resultant Gtetans were emerging with passion-satisfied languor from the tank of salt water.

As a measure of L'payr's depravity, let me pass on to you what the Gtetan police told me. Not only was he peddling the stuff to ameboid minors, but they believed that he had taken the photographs himself and that the model had been his own brother—or should I say sister? His own one and only sibling, possibly? This case has many, many confusing aspects.

Blatch returned the last picture to L'payr and said, "Yes, I am interested in buying the group. How much?"

The Gtetan named his price in terms of the requisite compounds available in the chemistry laboratory of the high school where Blatch taught. He explained exactly how he wanted them to be prepared and warned Blatch to tell nobody of L'payr's existence.

"Uzzerwise, when M'sieu gets 'ere tomorrow night, ze peekshures weel be gone, I weel be gone—and M'sieu weel have nozzing to show for his trouble. *Comprenez?*"

Osborne Blatch seems to have had very little trouble in obtaining and preparing the stuff for which L'payr had bargained. He said that, by the standards of his community, it was a minute quantity and extremely inexpensive. Also, as he had scrupulously always done in the past when using school supplies for his own experiments, he reimbursed the laboratory out of his own pocket. But he does admit that the photographs were only a small part of what he hoped to get out of the ameboid. He expected, once a sound business arrangement had been established, to find out from which part of the Solar System the visitor had come, what his world was like and similar matters of understandable interest to a creature whose civilization is in the late phases of Secretly Supervised Status.

Once the exchange had been effected, however, L'payr tricked him. The Gtetan told Blatch to return on the *next* night when, his time being more free, they could discuss the state of the Universe at leisure. And, of course, as soon as the Earthman had left with the photographs, L'payr jammed the fuel into his converters, made the necessary sub-nuclear rearrangements in its atomic structure and, with the hyperspace-drive once more operating under full power, took off like a *rilg* out of *Gowkuldady*.

As far as we can determine, Blatch received the deception philosophically. After all, he still had the pictures.

When my OP office was informed that L'payr had left Earth in the direction of the Hercules Cluster M13, without leaving any discernible ripple in terrestrial law or technology behind him, we all relaxed gratefully. The case was removed from TOP PRIORITY—FULL ATTENTION BY ALL PERSONNEL rating and placed in the PENDING LATENT EFFECTS category.

As is usual, I dropped the matter myself and gave full charge of the follow-up to my regent and representative on Earth, Stellar Corporal Pah-Chi-Luh. A tracer beam was put on L'payr's rapidly receding ship and I was free to devote my attention once more to my basic problem—delaying the development of interplanetary travel until the various human societies had matured to the requisite higher level.

Thus, six Earth months later, when the case broke wide open, Pah-Chi-Luh handled it himself and didn't bother me until the complications became overwhelming. I know this doesn't absolve me—I have ultimate responsibility for everything that transpires in my Outlying Patrol District. But between relatives, Hoy, I am mentioning these facts to show that I was not completely clumsy in the situation and that a little help from you and the rest of the family, when the case reaches the Old One in Galactic Headquarters, would not merely be charity for a one-headed oafish cousin.

As a matter of fact, I and most of my office were involved in a very complex problem. A Moslem mystic, living in Saudi Arabia, had attempted to heal the ancient schism that exists in his religion between the Shiite and Sunnite sects, by communing with the departed spirits of Mohammed's son-in-law, Ali, the patron of the first group, and Abu Bekr, the Prophet's father-in-law and founder of the Sunnite dynasty. The object of the mediumistic excursion was to effect some sort of arbitration agreement in Paradise between the two feuding ghosts that would

determine who should rightfully have been Mohammed's successor and the first caliph of Mecca.

Nothing is simple on Earth. In the course of this laudable probe of the hereafter, the earnest young mystic accidentally achieved telepathic contact with a Stage 9 civilization of disembodied intellects on Ganymede, the largest satellite of the planet Jupiter. Well, you can imagine! Tremendous uproar on Ganymede and in Saudi Arabia, pilgrims in both places flocking to see the individuals on either end of the telepathic connection, peculiar and magnificent miracles being wrought daily. A mess!

And my office feverishly working overtime to keep the whole affair simple and religious, trying to prevent it from splashing over into awareness of the more rational beings in each community! It's an axiom of Outlying Patrol Offices that nothing will stimulate space travel among backward peoples faster than definite knowledge of the existence of intelligent celestial neighbors. Frankly, if Pah-Chi-Luh had come to me right then, blathering of Gtetan pornography in human high-school textbooks, I'd probably have bitten his heads off.

He'd discovered the textbooks in the course of routine duties as an investigator for a United States Congressional Committee—his disguised status for the last decade or so, and one which had proved particularly valuable in the various delaying actions we had been surreptitiously fighting on the continent of North America. There was this newly published biology book, written for use in the secondary schools, which had received extremely favorable comment from outstanding scholars in the universities. Naturally, the committee ordered a copy of the text and suggested that its investigator look through it.

Corporal Pah-Chi-Luh turned a few pages and found himself staring at the very pornographic pictures he'd heard about at the briefing session six months before—published, available to everyone on Earth, and especially to minors! He told me afterward, brokenly, that in that instant all he saw was a brazen repetition of L'payr's ugly crime on his home planet.

He blasted out a Galaxy-wide alarm for the Gtetan.

L'payr had begun life anew as an *ashkebac* craftsman

87

on a small, out-of-the-way, mildly civilized world. Living carefully within the law, he had prospered and, at the time of his arrest, had become sufficiently conventional—and, incidentally, fat—to think of raising a respectable family. Not much—just two of him. If things continued to go well, he might consider multiple fission in the future.

He was indignant when he was arrested and carried off to the detention cell on Pluto, pending the arrival of an extradition party from Gtet.

"By what right do you disturb a peace-loving artisan in the quiet pursuit of his trade?" he challenged. "I demand immediate unconditional release, a full apology and restitution for loss of income as well as the embarrassment caused to my person and ego. Your superiors will hear of this! False arrest of a galactic citizen can be a very serious matter!"

"No doubt," Stellar Corporal Pah-Chi-Luh retorted, still quite equable, you see. "But the public dissemination of recognized pornography is even more serious. As a crime, we consider it on a level with—"

"*What* pornography?"

My assistant said he stared at L'payr for a long time through the transparent cell wall, marveling at the creature's effrontery. All the same, he began to feel a certain disquiet. He had never before encountered such complete self-assurance in the face of a perfect structure of criminal evidence.

"You know very well what pornography. Here—examine it for yourself. This is only one copy out of 20,000 distributed all over the United States of North America for the specific use of human adolescents." He dematerialized the biology text and passed it through the wall.

L'payr glanced at the pictures. "Bad reproduction," he commented. "Those humans still have a long way to go in many respects. However, they do display a pleasing technical precocity. But why show this to me? Surely you don't think *I* have anything to do with it?"

Pah-Chi-Luh says the Gtetan seemed intensely puzzled, yet gently patient, as if he were trying to unravel the hysterical gibberings of an idiot child.

"Do you *deny* it?"

"What in the Universe is there to deny? Let me see." He turned to the title page. "This seems to be *A First Book in Biology* by one Osborne Blatch and one Nicodemus P. Smith. You haven't mistaken me for either Blatch or Smith, have you? My name is L'payr, not Osborne L'payr, nor even Nicodemus P. L'payr. Just plain, old, everyday, simple L'payr. No more, no less. I come from Gtet, which is the sixth planet of—"

"I am fully aware of Gtet's astrographic location," Pah-Chi-Luh informed him coldly. "Also, that you were on Earth six of their months ago. And that, at the time, you completed a transaction with this Osborne Blatch, whereby you got the fuel you needed to leave the planet, while Blatch obtained the set of pictures that were later used as illustrations in that textbook. Our undercover organization on Earth functions very efficiently, as you can see. We have labeled the book Exhibit A."

"An ingenious designation," said the Gtetan admiringly. "Exhibit A! With so much to choose from, you picked the one that sounds just right. My compliments." He was, you will understand, Hoy, in his element—he was dealing with a police official on an abstruse legal point. L'payr's entire brilliant criminal past on a law-despising world had prepared him for this moment. Pah-Chi-Luh's mental orientation, however, had for a long time now been chiefly in the direction of espionage and *sub rosa* cultural manipulation. He was totally unprepared for the orgy of judicial quibbles that was about to envelop him. In all fairness to him, let me admit that I might not have done any better under those circumstances and neither, for that matter, might you—nor the Old One himself!

L'payr pointed out, "All I did was to sell a set of artistic studies to one Osborne Blatch. What *he* did with it afterward surely does not concern me. If I sell a weapon of approved technological backwardness to an Earthman—a flint fist-axe, say, or a cauldron for pouring boiling oil upon the stormers of walled cities—and he uses the weapon to dispatch one of his fellow primitives, am I culpable? Not the way I read the existing statutes of the Galactic Federation, my friend. Now suppose you reimburse me for my time and trouble and put me on a fast ship bound for my place of business."

Around and around they went. Dozens of times, Pah-Chi-Luh, going frantically through the Pluto Headquarters law library, would come up with a nasty little wrinkle of an ordinance, only to have L'payr point out that the latest interpretation of the Supreme Council put him wholly in the clear. I can myself vouch for the fact that the Gtetans seem to enjoy total recall of all judicial history.

"But you *do* admit selling pornography yourself to the Earthman Osborne Blatch?" the stellar corporal bellowed at last.

"Pornography, pornography," L'payr mused. "That would be defined as cheaply exciting lewdness, falsely titillating obscenity. Correct?"

"Of course!"

"Well, Corporal, let me ask you a question. You saw those pictures. Did you find them exciting or titillating?"

"Certainly not. But I don't happen to be a Gtetan ameboid."

"Neither," L'payr countered quietly, "is Osborne Blatch."

I do think Corporal Pah-Chi-Luh might have found some sensible way out of the dilemma if the extradition party had not just then arrived from Gtet on the special Patrol ship which had been sent for it. He now found himself confronted with six more magnificently argumentative ameboids, numbering among them some of the trickiest legal minds on the home planet. The police of Rugh VI had had many intricate dealings with L'payr in the Gtetan courts. Hence, they took no chances and sent their best representatives.

Outnumbered L'payr may have been, but remember, Hoy, he had prepared for just these eventualities ever since leaving Earth. And just to stimulate his devious intellect to maximum performance, there was the fact that *his* was the only life at stake. Once let his fellow ameboids get their pseudopods on him again, and he was a gone protozoan.

Between L'payr and the Gtetan extradition party, Corporal Pah-Chi-Luh began to find out how unhappy a policeman's lot can become. Back and forth he went, from the prisoner to the lawyers, stumbling through quagmires of opinion, falling into chasms of complexity.

The extradition group was determined not to return to their planet empty-pseudopoded. In order to succeed, they had to make the current arrest stick, which would give them the right—as previously injured parties—to assert their prior claim to the punishment of L'payr. For his part, L'payr was equally determined to invalidate the arrest by the Patrol, since then he would not only have placed our outfit in an uncomfortable position, but, no longer extraditable, would be entitled to its protection from his fellow citizens.

A weary, bleary and excessively hoarse Pah-Chi-Luh finally dragged himself to the extradition party on spindly tentacles and informed them that, after much careful consideration, he had come to the conclusion that L'payr was innocent of any crime during his stay on Earth.

"Nonsense," he was told by the spokesman. "A crime was committed. Arrant and unquestioned pornography was sold and circulated on that planet. A crime *has* to have been committed."

Pah-Chi-Luh went back to L'payr and asked, miserably, how about it? Didn't it seem, he almost pleaded, that all the necessary ingredients of a crime were present? *Some* kind of crime?

"True," L'payr said thoughtfully. "They have a point. Some kind of crime *may* have been committed—but not by me. Osborne Blatch, now . . ."

Stellar Corporal Pah-Chi-Luh completely lost his heads.

He sent a message to Earth, ordering Osborne Blatch to be picked up.

Fortunately for all of us, up to and including the Old One, Pah-Chi-Luh did not go so far as to have Blatch arrested. The Earthman was merely held as a material witness. When I think what the false arrest of a creature from a Secretly Supervised world could lead to, especially in a case of this sort, Hoy, my blood almost turns liquid.

But Pah-Chi-Luh *did* commit the further blunder of

incarcerating Osborne Blatch in a cell adjoining L'payr's. Everything, you will observe, was working out to the ameboid's satisfaction—including my young assistant.

By the time Pah-Chi-Luh got around to Blatch's first interrogation, the Earthman had already been briefed by his neighbor. Not that the briefing was displayed over-much—as yet.

"Pornography?" he repeated in answer to the first question. "*What* pornography? Mr. Smith and I had been working on an elementary biology text for some time and we were hoping to use new illustrations throughout. We wanted larger, clear pictures of the sort that would be instantly comprehensible to youngsters—and we were particularly interested in getting away from the blurry drawings that have been used and re-used in all textbooks, almost from the time of Leeuwenhoek. Mr. L'payr's series on the cycle of ameboid reproduction was a godsend. In a sense, they *made* the first section of the book."

"You don't deny, however," Corporal Pah-Chi-Luh inquired remorselessly, "that, at the time of the purchase, you knew those pictures were pornographic? And that, despite this knowledge, you went ahead and used them for the delectation of juveniles of your race?"

"Edification," the elderly human schoolteacher corrected him. "*Edification*, not delectation. I assure you that not a single student who studied the photographs in question—which, by the way, appeared textually as drawings—received any premature erotic stimulation thereby. I will admit that, at the time of purchase, I did receive a distinct impression from the gentleman in the next cell that he and his kind considered the illustrations rather racy—"

"Well, then?"

"But that was his problem, not mine. After all, if I buy an artifact from an extraterrestrial creature—a flint fist-axe, say, or a cauldron for pouring boiling oil upon the stormers of walled cities—and I use them both in completely peaceful and useful pursuits—the former to grub onions out of the ground and the latter to cook the onions in a kind of soup—have I done anything wrong?

"As a matter of fact, the textbook in question received

92

fine reviews and outstanding commendations from educational and scientific authorities all over the nation. Would you like to hear some of them? I believe I may have a review or two in my pockets. Let me see. Yes, just by chance, I seem to have a handful of clippings in this suit. Well, well! I didn't know there were quite so many. This is what the *Southern Prairie States Secondary School Gazette* has to say — 'A substantial and noteworthy achievement. It will live long in the annals of elementary science pedagoguery. The authors may well feel . . .'"

It was then that Corporal Pah-Chi-Luh sent out a despairing call for me.

Fortunately, I was free to give the matter my full attention, the Saudi Arabia-Ganymede affair being completely past the danger point. Had I been tied up . . .

After experimenting with all kinds of distractions, including secret agents disguised as dancing girls, we had finally managed to embroil the young mystic in a tremendous theological dispute on the exact nature and moral consequences of the miracles he was wreaking. Outstanding Mohammedan religious leaders of the region had lined up on one side or the other and turned the air blue with quotations from the Koran and later Sunnite books. The mystic was drawn in and became so involved in the argument that he stopped thinking about his original objectives and irreparably broke the mental connection with Ganymede.

For a while, this left a continuing problem on that satellite—it looked as if the civilization of disembodied intellects might eventually come to some approximation of the real truth. Luckily for us, the entire business had been viewed there also as a religious phenomenon and, once telepathic contact was lost, the intellect who had been communicating with the human, and had achieved much prestige thereby, was thoroughly discredited. It was generally believed that he had willfully and deliberately faked the entire thing, for the purpose of creating skepticism among the more spiritual members of his race. An ecclesiastical court ordered the unfortunate telepath to be embodied alive.

It was, therefore, with a warm feeling of a job well

done that I returned to my headquarters on Pluto in response to Pah-Chi-Luh's summons.

Needless to say, this feeling quickly changed to the most overpowering dismay. After getting the background from the overwrought corporal, I interviewed the Gtetan extradition force. They had been in touch with their home office and were threatening a major galactic scandal if the Patrol's arrest of L'payr was not upheld and L'payr remanded to their custody.

"Are the most sacred and intimate details of our sex life to be shamelessly flaunted from one end of the Universe to the other?" I was asked angrily. "Pornography is pornography—a crime is a crime. The intent was there —the overt act was there. We demand our prisoner."

"How can you have pornography without titillation?" L'payr wanted to know. "If a Chumblostian sells a Gtetan a quantity of *krrgllwss*—which they use as food and we use as building material—does the shipment have to be paid for under the nutritive or structural tariffs? The structural tariffs obtain, as you well know, Sergeant. I demand immediate release!"

But the most unpleasant surprise of all awaited me with Blatch. The terrestrial was sitting in his cell, sucking the curved handle of his umbrella.

"Under the code governing the treatment of all races on Secretly Supervised Status," he began as soon as he saw me, "and I refer not only to the Rigellian-Sagittarian Convention, but to the statutes of the third cosmic cycle and the Supreme Council decisions in the cases of Khwomo vs. Khwomo and Farziplok vs. Antares XII, I demand return to my accustomed habitat on Earth, the payment of damages according to the schedule developed by the Nobri Commission in the latest Vivadin controversy. I also demand satisfaction in terms of—"

"You seem to have acquired a good deal of knowledge of interstellar law," I commented slowly.

"Oh, I have, Sergeant—I have. Mr. L'payr was most helpful in acquainting me with my rights. It seems that I am entitled to all sorts of recompenses—or, at least, that I can claim entitlement. You have a very interesting galactic culture, Sergeant. Many, many people on Earth would be fascinated to learn about it. But I am quite prepared to spare you the embarrassment which such publicity would cause you. I am certain that two reasonable individuals like ourselves can come to terms."

When I charged L'payr with violating galactic secrecy, he spread his cytoplasm in an elaborate ameboid shrug.

"*I told him nothing on Earth*, Sergeant. Whatever information this terrestrial has received—and I will admit that it would have been damaging and highly illegal—was entirely in the jurisdiction of *your* headquarters office. Besides, having been wrongfully accused of an ugly and unthinkable crime, I surely had the right to prepare my defense by discussing the matter with the only witness to the deed. I might go further and point out that, since Mr. Blatch and myself are in a sense co-defendants, there could be no valid objection to a pooling of our legal knowledge."

Back in my office, I brought Corporal Pah-Chi-Luh up to date.

"It's like a morass," he complained. "The more you struggle to get out, the deeper you fall in it! And this terrestrial! The Plutonian natives who've been guarding him have been driven almost crazy. He asks questions about everything—what's this, what's that, how does it work. Or it's not hot enough for him, the air doesn't smell right, his food is uninteresting. His throat has developed an odd tickle, he wants a gargle, he needs a—"

"Give him everything he wants, but within reason," I said. "If this creature dies on us, you and I will be lucky to draw no more than a punishment tour in the Black Hole in Cygnus. But as for the rest of it—look here, Corporal, I find myself in agreement with the extradition party from Gtet. A crime *has* to have been committed."

Stellar Corporal Pah-Chi-Luh stared at me. "You— you mean . . ."

"I mean that if a crime was committed, L'payr has been legally arrested and can therefore be taken back to Gtet. We will then hear no more from him ever and we will also be rid of that bunch of pseudopod-clacking Gtetan shysters. That will leave us with only one problem—Osborne Blatch. Once L'payr is gone and we have this terrestrial to ourselves, I think we can handle him—one way or another. But first and foremost, Corporal Pah-Chi-Luh, a crime—*some crime*—has to have been committed by L'payr during his sojourn on Earth. Set up your bed in the law library."

Shortly afterward, Pah-Chi-Luh left for Earth.

Now please, Hoy, no moralistic comments! You know as well as I do that this sort of thing has been done before, here and there, in Outlying Patrol Offices. I don't like it any more than you, but I was faced with a major emergency. Besides, there was no doubt but that this L'payr, ameboid master criminal, had had punishment deferred far too long. In fact, one might say that morally I was completely and absolutely in the right.

Pah-Chi-Luh returned to Earth, as I've said, this time disguised as an editorial assistant. He got a job in the publishing house that had brought out the biology textbook. The original photographs were still in the files of that establishment. By picking his man carefully and making a good many mind-stimulating comments, the stellar corporal finally inspired one of the technical editors to examine the photographs and have the material on which they were printed analyzed.

The material was *fahrtuch*, a synthetic textile much in use on Gtet and not due to be developed by humanity for at least three centuries.

In no time at all, almost every woman in America was wearing lingerie made of *fahrtuch*, the novelty fabric of the year. And since L'payr was ultimately responsible for this illegal technological spurt, we at last had him where we wanted him!

He was very sporting about it, Hoy.

"The end of a long road for me, Sergeant. I congratulate you. Crime does not pay. Lawbreakers always lose. Law-enforcers always win."

I went off to prepare the extradition forms, without a care in the Galaxy. There was Blatch, of course, but he was a mere human. And by this time, having gotten involved in all kinds of questionable dealings myself, I was determined to make quick work of him. After all, one might as well get blasted for a *skreek* as a *launt!*

But when I returned to escort the Gtetan to his fellow-ameboids, I almost fell through the surface of Pluto. Where there had been one L'payr, there were now two! Smaller L'payrs, of course—half the size of the original, to be exact—but L'payrs unmistakable.

In the interval, he had reproduced!

How? That gargle the Earthman had demanded, Hoy. It had been L'payr's idea all along, his last bit of insurance. Once the Earthman had received the gargle, he had smuggled it to L'payr, who had hidden it in his cell, intending to use it as a last resort.

That gargle. Hoy, was *salt water!*

So there I was. The Gtetans informed me that their laws covered such possibilities, but much help *their* laws were to me.

"A crime has been committed, pornography has been sold," the spokesman reiterated. "We demand our prisoner. Both of him!"

"Pursuant to Galactic Statutes 6,009,371 through 6,106,514," Osborne Blatch insisted, "I demand immediate release, restitution to the extent of two billion Galactic Megawhars, a complete and written—"

And.

"It's probably true that our ancestor, L'payr, committed all sorts of indiscretions," lisped the two young ameboids in the cell next to Osborne Blatch, "but what does that have to do with us? L'payr paid for his crimes by dying in childbirth. We are very young and very, very innocent. Surely the big old Galaxy doesn't believe in punishing little children for the sins of their parents!"

What would *you* have done?

I shipped the whole mess off to Patrol Headquarters —the Gtetan extradition party and their mess of judicial citations, Osborne Blatch and his umbrella, the biology textbook, the original bundle of pornographic pictures, and last but not at all least, two—count 'em, two—dewy young ameboids. Call them L'payr sub-one and L'payr sub-two. Do anything you like with them when they get there, but please don't tell me what it is!

And if you can figure out a solution with the aid of some of the more ancient and wiser heads at headquarters, and figure it out before the Old One ruptures a gloc-cistomorph, Pah-Chi-Luh and I will be pathetically, eternally grateful.

If not—well, we're standing by here at Outlying Patrol Office 1001625 with bags packed. There's a lot to be said for the Black Hole in Cygnus.

Personally, Hoy, I'd say that the whole trouble is caused by creatures who insist on odd and colorful methods of continuing their race, instead of doing it sanely and decently by means of spore-pod explosion!

THE FLAT-EYED MONSTER

FOR THE first few moments, Clyde Manship—who up to then had been an assistant professor of Comparative Literature at Kelly University—for the first few moments, Manship tried heroically to convince himself that he was merely having a bad dream. He shut his eyes and told himself chidingly, with a little superior smile playing about his lips, that things as ugly as this just did not occur in real life. No. Definitely a dream.

He had himself half convinced, until he sneezed. It was too loud and wet a sneeze to be ignored. You didn't sneeze like that in a dream—if you sneezed at all. He gave up. He'd have to open his eyes and take another look. At the thought, his neck muscles went rigid with spasm.

A little while ago, he'd fallen asleep while reading an article he'd written for a scholarly journal. He'd fallen asleep in his own bed in his own apartment in Callahan Hall—"a charming and inexpensive residence for those members of the faculty who are bachelors and desire to live on campus." He'd awakened with a slightly painful tingling sensation in every inch of his body. He felt as if he were being stretched, stretched interminably and—and *loosened*. Then, abruptly, he had floated off the bed and gone through the open window like a rapidly attentuating curl of smoke. He'd gone straight up to the star-drenched sky of night, dwindling in substance until he lost consciousness completely.

And had come to on this enormous flat expanse of white table-top, with a multi-vaulted ceiling above him and dank, barely breathable air in his lungs. Hanging from the ceiling were quantities and quantities of what was indubitably electronic equipment, but the kind of equipment the boys in the Physics Department might dream up, if the grant they'd just received from the government for military radiation research had been a million times larger than it was, and if Professor Bowles, the department head, had insisted that every gadget be carefully constructed to look substantially different from anything done in electronics to date.

The equipment above him had been rattling and gurgling and whooshing, glowing and blinking and coruscating. Then it had stopped as if someone had been satisfied and had turned off a switch.

So Clyde Manship had sat up to see who had turned it off.

He had seen all right.

He hadn't seen so much *who* as he had seen *what*. And it hadn't been a nice *what*. In fact, none of the *whats* he had glimpsed in that fast look around had been a bit nice. So he had shut his eyes fast and tried to find another mental way out of the situation.

But now he had to have another look. It might not be so bad the second time. "It's always darkest," he told himself with determined triteness, "before the dawn." And then found himself involuntarily adding, "Except on days when there's an eclipse."

But he opened his eyes anyway, wincingly, the way a child opens its mouth for the second spoonful of castor oil.

Yes, they were all as he had remembered them. Pretty awful.

The table-top was an irregular sort of free-form shape, bordered by thick, round knobs a few inches apart. And perched on these knobs, about six feet to the right of him, were two creatures who looked like black leather suitcases. Instead of handles or straps, however, they sported a profusion of black tentacles, dozens and dozens of tentacles, every second or third one of which ended in a moist turquoise eye shielded by a pair of the sweepingest eyelashes Manship had ever seen outside of a mascara advertisement.

Imbedded in the suitcase proper, as if for additional decorative effect, were swarms of other sky-blue eyes, only these, without eyelashes, bulged out in multitudes of tiny, glittering facets like enormous gems. There was no sign of ear, nose or mouth anywhere on the bodies, but there was a kind of slime, a thick, grayish slime, that oozed out of the black bodies and dripped with a steady splash-splash-splash to the floor beneath.

On his left, about fifteen feet away, where the table-top extended a long peninsula, there was another one of the creatures. Its tentacles gripped a pulsating spheroid across the surface of which patches of light constantly appeared and disappeared.

As near as Manship could tell, all the visible eyes of the three were watching him intently. He shivered and tried to pull his shoulders closer together.

"Well, Professor," someone asked suddenly, "what would you say?"

"I'd say this was one hell of a way to wake up," Manship burst out, feelingly. He was about to go on and develop this theme in more colorful detail when two things stopped him.

The first was the problem of who had asked the question. He had seen no other human—no other living creature, in fact—besides the three tentacled suitcases anywhere in that tremendous, moisture-filled room.

The second thing that stopped him was that someone else had begun to answer the question at the same time, cutting across Manship's words and ignoring them completely.

"Well, obviously," this person said, "the experiment is a success. It has completely justified its expense and the long years of research behind it. You can see for yourself, Councilor Glomg, that one-way teleportation is an accomplished fact."

100

Manship realized that the voices were coming from his right. The wider of the two suitcases—evidently "the professor" to whom the original query had been addressed—was speaking to the narrower one who had swung most of his stalked eyes away from Manship and had focused them on his companion. Only where in blazes were the voices coming from? Somewhere inside their bodies? There was no sign anywhere of vocal apparatus.

AND HOW COME, Manship's mind suddenly shrieked, THEY TALK ENGLISH?

"I can see that," Councilor Glomg admitted with a blunt honesty that became him well. "It's an accomplished fact, all right, Professor Lirld. Only, *what precisely* has it accomplished?"

Lirld raised some thirty or forty tentacles in what Manship realized fascinatedly was an elaborate and impatient shrug. "The teleportation of a living organism from astronomical unit 649-301-3 without the aid of transmitting apparatus on the planet of origin."

The Councilor swept his eyes back to Manship. "You call that living?" he inquired doubtfully.

"Oh, come now, Councilor," Professor Lirld protested. "Let's not have any flefnomorphism. It is obviously sentient, obviously motile, after a fashion—"

"All right. It's alive. I'll grant that. But sentient? It doesn't even seem to *pmbff* from where I stand. And those horrible lonely eyes! Just two of them—and so *flat!* That dry, dry skin without a trace of slime. I'll admit that—"

"You're not exactly a thing of beauty and a joy forever yourself, you know," Manship, deeply offended, couldn't help throwing out indignantly.

"—I tend to flefnomorphism in my evaluation of alien life-forms," the other went on as if he hadn't spoken. "Well, I'm a flefnobe and proud of it. But after all, Professor Lirld, I have seen some impossible creatures from our neighboring planets that my son and other explorers have brought back. The very strangest of them, the most primitive ones, at least can *pmbff!* But this—this *thing*. Not the smallest, slightest trace of a *pmb* do I see on it! It's eerie, that's what it is—eerie!"

101

"Not at all," Lirld assured him. "It's merely a scientific anomaly. Possibly in the outer reaches of the Galaxy where animals of this sort are frequent, possibly conditions are such that *pmbffing* is unnecessary. A careful examination should tell us a good deal very quickly. Meanwhile, we've proved that life exists in other areas of the Galaxy than its sun-packed core. And when the time comes for us to conduct exploratory voyages to these areas, intrepid adventurers like your son will go equipped with information. They will know what to expect."

"Now, listen," Manship began shouting in desperation. "Can you or can you not hear me?"

"You can shut off the power, Srin," Professor Lirld commented. "No sense in wasting it. I believe we have as much of this creature as we need. If any more of it is due to materialize, it will arrive on the residual beam."

The flefnobe on Manship's left rapidly spun the strange spheroid he was holding. A low hum, which had filled the building and had been hardly noticeable before, now died away. As Srin peered intently at the patches of light on the surface of the instrument, Manship suddenly guessed that they were meter readings. Yes, that's exactly what they were—meter readings. *Now, how did I know that?* he wondered.

Obvious. There was only one answer. If they couldn't hear him no matter how loudly he shouted, if they gave no sign that they even knew he *was* shouting, and if, at the same time, they seemed to indulge in the rather improbable feat of talking his native language—they were obviously telepaths. Without anything that looked like ears or mouths.

He listened carefully as Srin asked his superior a question. It seemed to sound in his ears as words, English words in a clear, resonant voice. But there was a difference. There was a quality missing, the kind of realistic bite that fresh fruit has and artificial fruit flavoring doesn't. And behind Srin's words there were low, murmuring bubbles of other words, unorganized sentence fragments which would occasionally become "audible" enough to clarify a subject that was not included in the "conversation." That, Manship realized, was how he had learned that the shifting patches of light on the spheroid were meter readings.

It was also evident that whenever they mentioned something for which no equivalent at all existed in English, his mind supplied him with a nonsense syllable.

So far so good. He'd been plucked out of his warm bed in Callahan Hall by a telepathic suitcase named something like Lirld which was equipped with quantities of eyes and tentacles. He'd been sucked down to some planet in an entirely different system near the center of the Galaxy, clad in nothing but apple-green pajamas.

H was on a world of telepaths who couldn't hear him at all, but upon whom he could eavesdrop with ease, his brain evidently being a sufficiently sensitive antenna. He was scheduled shortly to undergo a "careful examination," a prospect he did not relish, the more so as he was evidently looked upon as a sort of monstrous laboratory animal. Finally, he was not thought much of, chiefly because he couldn't *pmbff* worth a damn.

All in all, Clyde Manship decided, it was about time that he made his presence felt. Let them know, so to speak, that he was definitely not a lower form of life, but one of the boys. That he belonged to the mind-over-matter club himself and came of a long line of IQ-fanciers on both sides of his family.

Only *how?*

Vague memories of adventure stories read as a boy drifted back to him. Explorers land on a strange island. Natives, armed with assorted spears, clubs and small boulders, gallop out of the jungle to meet them, their whoops an indisputable prelude to mayhem. Explorers, sweating a bit, as they do not know the language of this particular island, must act quickly. Naturally, they resort to—they resort to—the universal sign language! *Sign* language. Universal!

Still in a sitting position, Clyde Manship raised both arms straight up over his head. "Me *friend*," he intoned. "Me come in peace." He didn't expect the dialogue to get across, but it seemed to him that voicing such words might help him psychologically and thus add more sincerity to the gesture.

"—and you might as well turn off the recording apparatus, too," Professor Lirld was instructing his assistant. "From here on out, we'll take everything down on a double memory-fix."

Srin manipulated his spheroid again. "Think I should modulate the dampness, sir? The creature's dry skin seems to argue a desert climate."

"Not at all. I strongly suspect it to be one of those primitive forms which can survive in a variety of environments. The specimen seems to be getting along admirably. I tell you, Srin, we can be very well satisfied with the results of the experiment up to this point."

"Me friend," Manship went on desperately, raising and lowering his arms. "Me intelligent entity. Me have I.Q. of 140 on the Wechsler-Bellevue scale."

"*You* may be satisfied," Glomg was saying, as Lirld left the table with a light jump and floated, like an oversized dandelion, to a mass of equipment overhead, "but I'm not. I don't like this business one little bit."

"Me friendly *and* intelligent enti—" Manship began. He sneezed again. "Damn this wet air," he muttered morosely.

"What was *that?*" Glomg demanded.

"Nothing very important, Councilor," Srin assured him. "The creature did it before. It is evidently a low-order biological reaction that takes place periodically, possibly a primitive method of imbibing *glrnk*. Not by any stretch of the imagination a means of communication, however."

"I wasn't thinking of communication," Glomg observed testily. "I thought it might be a prelude to aggressive action."

The professor skimmed back to the table, carrying a skein of luminescent wires. "Hardly. What could a creature of this sort be aggressive *with?* I'm afraid you're letting your mistrust of the unknown run away with you, Councilor Glomg."

Manship had crossed his arms across his chest and subsided into a helpless silence. There was evidently no way to make himself understood outside of telepathy. And how do you start transmitting telepathically for the first time? What do you use?

If only his doctoral thesis had been in biology or physiology, he thought wistfully, instead of *The Use of the Second Aorist in the First Three Books of the Iliad*. Oh, well. He was a long way from home. Might as well try.

He closed his eyes, having first ascertained that Professor Lirld did not intend to approach his person with the new piece of equipment. He wrinkled his forehead and leaned forward with an effort of extreme concentration.

Testing, he thought as hard as he could, *testing, testing. One, two, three, four—testing, testing. Can you hear me?*

"I just don't like it," Glomg announced again. "I don't like what we're doing here. Call it a presentiment, call it what you will, but I feel we are tampering with the infinite—and we shouldn't."

I'm testing, Manship ideated frantically. *Mary had a little lamb. Testing, testing. I'm the alien creature and I'm trying to communicate with you. Come in, please.*

"Now, Councilor," Lirld protested irritably. "Let's have none of that. This is a scientific experiment."

"That's all very well. But I believe there are mysteries that flefnobe was never meant to examine. Monsters as awful looking as this—no slime on the skin, only two eyes and both of them flat, unable or unwilling to *pmbff*, an almost complete absence of tentacles—a creature of this sort should have been left undisturbed on its own hellish planet. There are limits to science, my learned friend—or there should be. One should not seek to know the unknowable!"

Can't you hear me? Manship begged. *Alien entity to Srin, Lirld and Glomg: This is an attempt at a telepathic connection. Come in, please, someone. Anyone.* He considered for a moment, then added: *Roger. Over.*

"I don't recognize such limitations, Councilor. My curiosity is as vast as the Universe."

"That may be," Glomg rejoined portentously. "But there are more things in *Tiz* and *Tetzbah*, Professor Lirld, than are dreamed of in your philosophy."

"My philosophy—" Lirld began, and broke off to announce—"Here's your son. Why don't you ask him? Without the benefit of half a dozen scientific investigations that people like you have wanted to call off time

105

after time, none of his heroic achievements in interplanetary discovery would be possible."

Thoroughly defeated, but still curious, Manship opened his eyes in time to see an extremely narrow black suitcase swarm up to the table-top in a spaghetti-cluster of tentacles.

"What is—*that?*" the newcomer inquired, curling a bunch of supercilious eye-stalks over Manship's head. "It looks like a *yurd* with a bad case of *hipplestatch.*" He considered for a moment, then added, "Galloping *hipplestatch.*"

"It's a creature from astronomical unit 649-301-3 that I've just succeeded in teleporting to our planet," Lirld told him proudly. "Mind you, Rabd, without a transmitting outfit on the other end! I admit I don't know why it worked this time and never before—but that's a matter for further research. A beautiful specimen, though, Rabd. And as near as we can tell, in perfect condition. You can put it away now, Srin."

"Oh, no you don't, Srin—" Manship had barely started to announce when a great rectangle of some pliable material fell from the ceiling and covered him. A moment later, the table-top on which he'd been sitting seemed to drop away and the ends of the material were gathered in underneath him and fastened with a click by a scuttling individual whom he took to be the assistant. Then, before he had time to so much as wave his arms, the table-top shot up with an abruptness that he found twice as painful as it was disconcerting.

And there he was, packaged as thoroughly as a birthday present. All in all, things were not improving, he decided. Well, at least they seemed disposed to leave him alone now. And as yet they showed no tendency to shove him up on a laboratory shelf along with dusty jars of flefnobe foetuses pickled in alcohol.

The fact that he was probably the first human being in history to make contact with an extraterrestrial race failed to cheer Clyde Manship in the slightest.

First, he reflected, the contact had been on a distinctly minor key—the sort that an oddly colored moth makes with a collector's bottle rather than a momentous meeting between the proud representatives of two different civilizations.

Second, and much more important, this sort of hands-across-the-cosmos affair was more likely to enthuse an astronomer, a sociologist or even a physicist than an assistant professor of Comparative Literature.

He'd had fantastic daydreams aplenty in his lifetime. But they concerned being present at the premiere of *Macbeth*, for example, and watching a sweating Shakespeare implore Burbage not to shout out the "Tomorrow and Tomorrow and Tomorrow" speech in the last act: "For God's sake, Dick, your wife just died and you're about to lose your kingdom and your life—don't let it sound like Meg at the Mermaid screaming for a dozen of ale. *Philosophical*, Dick, that's the idea, slow, mournful and philosophical. And just a little bewildered."

Or he'd imagined being one of the company at that moment sometime before 700 B.C. when a blind poet rose and intoned for the first time: "Anger, *extreme* anger, that is my tale . . ."

Or being a house guest at Yasnaya Polyana when Tolstoy wandered in from the garden with an abstracted look on his face and muttered: "Just got an idea for a terrific yarn about the Napoleonic invasion of Russia. And what a title! *War and Peace*. Nothing pretentious, nothing complicated. Just simply *War and Peace*. It'll knock them dead in St. Petersburg, I tell you. Of course, it's just a bare little short story at the moment, but I'll probably think of a couple of incidents to pad it out."

Travel to the Moon and the other planets of the Solar System let alone a voyage to the center of the Galaxy—in his pajamas? No, that was definitely not a menu calculated to make Clyde Manship salivate. In this respect, he had wisted no farther afield than a glimpse, say, of Victor Hugo's sky-high balcony in St. Germain de Près or the isles of Greece where burning Sappho loved and, from time to time as it occurred to her, sang.

Professor Bowles, now, Bowles or any of the other slip-stick-sniffers in the physics department—what those boys would give to be in his position! To be the subject of an actual experiment far beyond the dreams of even theory on Earth, to be exposed to a technology that was patently so much more advanced than theirs—why, they would probably consider that, in exchange for all this, the vivisection that Manship was morosely certain would end the evening's festivities was an excellent bargain and verged on privilege. The physics department . . .

Manship suddenly recalled the intricately weird tower, studded with gray dipoles, that the physics department had been erecting in Murphy field. He'd watched the government-subsidized project in radiation research going up from his window in Callahan Hall.

Only the evening before, when it had reached the height of his window, he'd reflected that it looked more like a medieval siege engine designed to bring down walled cities than a modern communicative device.

But now, with Lirld's comment about one-way teleportation never having worked before, he found himself wondering whether the uncompleted tower, poking a ragged section of electronic superstructure at his bedroom window, had been partially responsible for this veritable purée-of-nightmare he'd been wading through.

Had it provided a necessary extra link with Lirld's machine, sort of an aerial connection or grounding wire or whatever? If only he knew a little physics! Eight years of higher education were inadequate to suggest the barest aye or nay.

He gnashed his teeth, went too far and bit his tongue—and was forced to suspend mental operations until the pain died away and the tears dribbled out of his eyes.

What if he knew for certain that the tower had played a potent, though passive, part in his removal through interstellar space? What if he knew the exact part it had played in terms of megavolts and amperages and so forth —would the knowledge be the slightest use to him in this impossible situation?

No, he'd still be a hideous flat-eyed, non-intelligent monster plucked pretty much at random from the outer reaches of the Universe, surrounded by creatures to whose minds his substantial knowledge of the many literatures of astronomical unit 649-301-3 would probably come across, allowing even for the miracle of translation, as so much schizophrenic word-salad.

In his despair, he plucked hopelessly at the material in which he'd been wrapped. Two small sections came away in his fingers.

There wasn't enough light to examine them, but the feel was unmistakable. Paper. He was wrapped in an over-sized sheet of something very much like paper.

It made sense, he thought, it made sense in its own weird way. Since the appendages of the flefnobes he had seen to date consisted of nothing more than slender tentacles ending in either eyes or tapered points, and since they seemed to need knoblike protuberances on the laboratory table in order to perch beside him, a cage of paper was pretty much escape-proof from their point of view. There was nothing for their tentacles to grip—and they evidently didn't have the musculature to punch their way through.

Well, he did. Athletically, he had never amounted to much, but he believed, given enough of an emergency, in his ability to fight his way out of a paper bag. It was a comforting thought, but, at the moment, only slightly more useful than the nugget about the tower in Murphy Field.

If only there were some way of transmitting *that* bit of information to Lirld's little group: Maybe they'd realize that the current flefnobe version of *The Mindless Horror from Hyperspace* had a few redeeming intellectual qualities, and maybe they could work out a method of sending him back. If they wanted to.

Only he couldn't transmit information. All he could do, for some reason peculiar to the widely separate evolutionary paths of man and flefnobe, was receive. So former Assistant Professor Clyde Manship sighed heavily, slumped his shoulders yet a further slump—and stolidly set himself to receive.

He also straightened his pajamas about him tenderly, not so much from latent sartorial ambition as because of agonizing twinges of nostalgia: he had suddenly realized that the inexpensive green garment with its heavily standardized cut was the only artifact he retained of his own world. It was the single souvenir, so to speak, that he possessed of the civilization which had produced both Tamurlane and *Terza Rima;* the pajamas were, in fact, outside of his physical body, his last link with Earth.

"So far as I'm concerned," Glomg's explorer son was commenting—it was obvious that the argument had been breezing right along and that the papery barrier didn't affect Manship's "hearing" in the slightest—"I can take these alien monsters or leave them alone. When they get as downright disgusting as this, of course, I'd rather leave them alone. But what I mean—I'm not afraid of tampering with the infinite, like Pop here, and on the other side, I can't believe that what you're doing, Professor Lirld, will ever lead to anything really important."

He paused, then went on. "I hope I haven't hurt your feelings, sir, but that's what I honestly think. I'm a practical flefnobe, and I believe in practical things."

"How can you say—nothing really important?" In spite of Rabd's apology, the professor's mental "voice" as it registered on Manship's brain positively undulated with indignation. "Why, the greatest concern of flefnobe science at the moment is to achieve a voyage to some part of the outer Galaxy where the distances between stars are prodigious compared to their relative denseness here at the galactic center.

"We can travel at will between the fifty-four planets of our system and we have recently achieved flight to several of our neighboring suns, but going so far as even the middle areas of the Galaxy, where this specimen originates, remains as visionary a project today as it was before the dawn of extra-atmospheric flight over two centuries ago."

"Right!" Rabd broke in sharply. "And why? Because we don't have the ships capable of making the journey? Not on your *semble-swol*, Professor! Why, since the development of the *Bulvonn* Drive, any ship in the flefnobe navy or merchant marine, down to my little three-jet runabout, could scoot out to a place as far as astronomical unit 649-301-3—to name just one example—and back without even hotting up her engines. But we don't. And for a very good reason."

Clyde Manship was now listening—or receiving—so hard that the two halves of his brain seemed to grind against each other. He was very much interested in astronomical unit 649-301-3 and anything that made travel to it easier or more difficult, however exotic the method of transportation employed might be by prevailing terrestrial standards.

"And the reason, of course," the young explorer went on, "is a practical one. Mental dwindle. Good old mental dwindle. In two hundred years of solving every problem connected with space travel, we haven't so much as *pmbffed* the surface of *that* one. All we have to do is go a measly twenty light-years from the surface of our home planet and mental dwindle sets in with a bang. The brightest crews start acting like retarded children and, if they don't turn back right away, their minds go out like so many lights: they've dwindled mentally smack down to zero."

It figured, Manship decided excitedly, it figured. A telepathic race like the flefnobes . . . why, of course! Accustomed since earliest infancy to having the mental aura of the entire species about them at all times, dependent completely on telepathy for communication since there had never been a need for developing any other method, what loneliness, what ultimate magnification of loneliness, must they not feel once their ships had reached a point too far from their world to maintain contact!

And their education now—Manship could only guess at the educational system of a creature so different from himself, but surely it must be a kind of high-order and continual mental osmosis, a mutual mental osmosis. However it worked, their educational system probably accentuated the involvement of the individual with the group. Once the feeling of involvement became too tenuous, because of intervening barrier or overpowering stellar distance, the flefnobe's psychological disintegration was inevitable.

But all this was unimportant. There were interstellar space ships in existence! There were vehicles that could take Clyde Manship back to Earth, back to Kelly University and the work-in-progress he hoped would eventually

111

win him a full professorship in comparative literature: *Style vs. Content in Fifteen Representative Corporation Reports to Minority Stockholders for the Period* 1919-1931.

For the first time, hope sprang within his breast. A moment later, it was lying on its back and massaging a twisted knee. Because assume, just assume for the sake of argument, his native intelligence told him, that he could somehow get out of this place and pick his way about what was, by every indication, a complete oddity of a world, until he found the spaceships Rabd had mentioned —could it ever be believed by any imagination no matter how wild or fevered, his native intelligence continued, that he, Clyde Manship, whose fingers were all thumbs and whose thumbs were all knuckles, whose mechanical abilities would have made Swanscombe Man sneer and *Sinanthropus* snicker, could it ever be believed, his native intelligence inquired sardonically, that he'd be capable of working out the various gadgets of advanced spaceship design, let alone the peculiarities that highly unusual creatures like the flefnobes would inevitably have incorporated into their vessels?

Clyde Manship was forced to admit morosely that the entire project was somewhat less than possible. But he did tell his native intelligence to go straight to hell.

Rabd now, though. *Rabd* could pilot him back to Earth if (a) Rabd found it worth-while personally and if (b) Rabd could be communicated with. Well, what interested Rabd most? Evidently this Mental Dwindle ranked quite high.

"If you'd come up with an answer to that, Professor," he was expostulating at this point, "I would cheer so hard I'd unship my *glrnk*. That's what's kept us boxed up here at the center of the Galaxy for too many years. That's the *practical* problem. But when you haul this *Qrm*-forsaken blob of protoplasm out of its hole halfway across the Universe and ask me what I think of it, I must tell you the whole business leaves me completely dry. This, to me, is not a practical experiment."

Manship caught the mental ripples of a nod from Rabd's father. "I'm forced to agree with you, son. Impractical

112

and dangerous. And I think I can get the rest of the council to see it my way. Far too much has been spent on this project already."

As the resonance of their thoughts decreased slightly in volume, Manship deduced they were leaving the laboratory.

He heard the beginnings of a desperate, "But—but—" from Lirld. Then, off in the distance, Councilor Glomg, evidently having dismissed the scientist, asked his son a question, "And where is little Tekt? I thought she'd be with you."

"Oh, she's out at the landing field," Rabd answered, "supervising last-minute stuff going into the ship. After all, we begin our mating flight tonight."

"A wonderful female," Glomg told him in a "voice" that was now barely audible. "You're a very lucky flefnobe."

"I know that, Pop," Rabd assured him. "Don't think I don't know that. The most plentiful bunch of eye-ended tentacles this side of *Gansibokkle* and they're mine, all mine!"

"Tekt is a warm and highly intelligent female flefnobe," his father pointed out severely from a great distance. "She has many fine qualities. I don't like you acting as if the mating process were a mere matter of the number of eye-ended tentacles possessed by the female."

"Oh, it isn't, Pop," Rabd assured him. "It isn't at all. The mating process is a grave and—er, a serious matter to me. Full of responsibilities—er, serious responsibilities. Yes, sir. Highly serious. But the fact that Tekt has over a hundred and seventy-six slime-washed tentacles, each topped by a lovely, limpid eye, won't do our relationship a bit of harm. Quite the contrary, Pop, quite the contrary."

"A superstitious old crank and a brash bumpkin," Professor Lirld commented bitterly. "But between them, they can have my appropriation shut off, Srin. They can stop my work. Just when it's showing positive results. We've got to prepare countermeasures!"

Manship was not interested in this all-too-familiar academic despair, however. He was straining desperately

113

after the receding minds of Glomg and Rabd. Not that he was at all intrigued by the elder's advice on How to Have a Sane and Happy Sex Life though Married.

What had excited him prodigiously was a mental by-product of a much earlier comment. When Rabd had mentioned the last-minute loading of his ship, another part of the flefnobe's mind had, as if stimulated by association, dwelt briefly on the construction of the small vessel, its maintenance and, most important, its operation.

For just a few seconds, there had been a flash of a control panel with varicolored lights going on and off, and the beginnings of long-ago, often-repeated instruction: "To warm up the motors of the *Bulvonn* Drive, first gently rotate the uppermost three cylinders . . . Gently now!"

It was the kind of subliminal thought-picture, Manship realized excitedly, that had emanated from Srin a short while ago, and had enabled him to guess that the shifting light-patterns on the sphere the laboratory assistant held were actually meter readings. Evidently, his sensitivity to the flefnobe brain went deeper than the mental statements that were consciously transmitted by it and penetrated, if not the unconscious mind, at least the less submerged areas of personal awareness and memory.

But this meant—this meant—seated as he was, he still managed to stagger at the concept. A little practice, just a little acquired skill, and he could no doubt pick the brain of every flefnobe on the planet.

He sat and glowed at the thought. An ego that had never been particularly robust had been taking an especially ferocious pounding in the past half-hour under the contemptuous scrutiny of a hundred turquoise eyes and dozens of telepathic gibes. A personality that had been power-starved most of its adult life abruptly discovered it might well hold the fate of an entire planet in the hollow of its cerebrum.

Yes, this certainly made him feel a lot better. Every bit of information these flefnobes possessed was his for the taking. What, for example, did he feel like taking? For a starter, that is.

Manship remembered. His euphoria dwindled like a

spat-upon match. There was only one piece of information he desired, only one thing he wanted to know. How
to get home!

One of the few creatures on this planet, possibly the
only one for all he knew, whose thoughts were of a type
to make this possible, was on his way with his father to
some flefnobe equivalent of Tony's Bar and Grill. Rabd
had, in fact, to judge from the silence reigning on the subject, just this moment passed out of effective telepathic
range.

With a hoarse, anguished, yearning cry, similar to that
of a bull who—having got in a juicy lick with his horns
and having been carried by the momentum of his rush
the full length of the bull-ring—turns, only to see the
attendants dragging the wounded matador out of the
arena . . . with precisely that sort of thoroughly dismayed
bellow, Clyde Manship reached up, tore the surrounding
material apart with one mighty two-handed gesture, and
leaped to his feet on the in-and-out curving table-top.

". . . And seven or eight charts in full color, represent-
ing the history of teleportation prior to this experiment,"
Lirld was telling his assistant at that moment. "In fact,
Srin, if you have time to make *three-dimensional* charts,
the Council is even more likely to be impressed. We're in
a fight, Srin, and we've got to use every—"

His thoughts broke off as an eye-stalk curled around
and regarded Manship. A moment later his entire complement of eye-stalks as well as those of his assistant swished
about and stopped, quivering, with their focus on the
erect, emergent human.

"Holy, concentrated *Qrm*," the professor's mind barely
transmitted the quavering thought. "The flat-eyed monster. It's broken loose!"

"Out of a cage of solid paper!" Srin added in awe.

Lirld came to a decision. "The blaster," he ordered
peremptorily. "Tentacle me the blaster, Srin. Appropriation or no appropriation, we don't dare take chances with
a creature like this. We're in a crowded city. Once it got
out on a rampage—" He shuddered the entire black suitcase length of him. He made a rapid adjustment in the

115

curlicued instrument that Srin had given him. He pointed it at Manship.

Having actually fought his way out of the paper bag, Manship had paused, irresolute, on the table-top. Far from being a man of action in any sense, he now found himself distinctly puzzled as to just which way to act. He had no idea of the direction taken by Glomg *père* and *fils;* furthermore he was at a loss as he looked around for anything that in any way resembled a door. He regretted very much not having noticed through which aperture Rabd had entered the room upon the occasion of the younger flefnobe's joining their jolly little circle.

He had just about made up his mind to look into a series of zig-zag indentations in the opposite wall, when he observed Lirld pointing the blaster at him with determined if unprofessional tremulousness. His mind, which had been filing the recent conversation between professor and assistant in an uninterested back-portion, suddenly informed him that he was about to become the first, and probably unrecorded victim, in a War of Worlds.

"Hey!" he yelped, entirely forgetting his meager powers of communication. "I just want to look up Rabd. I'm not going on any ramp—"

Lirld did something to the curlicued instrument that seemed like winding a clock, but was probably more equivalent to the pressing of a trigger. He simultaneously shut all of his eyes—no mean feat in itself.

That, Clyde Manship reflected later—when there was time and space to reflect—was the only thing which saved his life. That and the prodigious sideways broad-jump he made as millions of crackling red dots ripped out of the instrument toward him.

The red dots sped past his pajama-tops and into one of the lower vaults that made up the ceiling. Without a sound, a hole some ten feet in circumference appeared in the masonry. The hole was deep enough—some three or four feet—to let the night sky of the planet show through. A heavy haze of white powder drifted down like the dust from a well-beaten rug.

Staring at it, Manship felt the roll of tiny glaciers to-

116

ward his heart. His stomach flattened out against its abdominal wall and tried to skulk quietly around his ribs. He had never felt so completely frightened in his life. "Hey-y-y—" he began.

"A little too much power, Professor," Srin observed judiciously from where he rested easily with tentacles outspread against the wall. "A little too much power and not enough *glrnk*. Try a little more *glrnk* and see what happens."

"Thank you," Lirld told him gratefully. "Like this, you mean?"

He raised and pointed the instrument again.

"Hey-y-y!" Manship continued in the same vein as before, not so much because he felt the results of such a statement would be particularly rewarding as because he lacked, at the moment, the creative faculties for another, more elaborate comment. "Hey-y-y-y!" he repeated between chattering teeth, staring at Lirld out of eyes no longer entirely flat.

He held up a shaking, admonishing hand. Fear was gibbering through him like the news of panic through a nation of monkeys. He watched the flefnobe make the peculiar winding trigger adjustment again. His thoughts came to a stop and every muscle in his body seemed to tense unendurably.

Suddenly Lirld shook. He slid backward along the table-top. The weapon dropped out of stiffened tentacles and smashed into bunches of circular wires that rolled in all directions. "Srin!" his mind whimpered. "Srin! The monster—Do—do you see what's coming out of his eyes? He's—he's—"

His body cracked open and a pale, blue goo poured out. Tentacles dropped off him like so many long leaves in a brisk autumn wind. The eyes that studded his surface turned from turquoise to a dull brown. "*Srin!*" he begged in a tiny, faraway thought. "Help me—the flat-eyed monster is—help—help!"

And then he dissolved. Where he had been, there was nothing but a dark liquid, streaked with blue, that flowed and bubbled and dripped off the curving edge of the table.

Manship stared at it uncomprehendingly, realizing only one thing fully—he was still alive.

A flicker of absolutely mad, stampeding fear reached him from Srin's mind. The laboratory assistant jumped from the wall against which he'd been standing, skidded across the table-top with thrashing tentacles, paused for a moment at the knobs that lined its edge to get the necessary traction—and then leaped in an enormous arc to the far wall of the building. The zig-zag indentations widened in a sort of lightning flash to let his body through.

So that *had* been a door after all. Manship found himself feeling rather smug at the deduction. With so little to go on—pretty smart, *pretty* smart.

And then the various parts of his brain caught up with current events and he began trembling from the reaction. He should be dead, a thing of shredded flesh and powdered bone. What had happened?

Lirld had fired the weapon at him and missed the first time. Just as he was about to fire again, something had struck the flefnobe about as hard as it had the Assyrian back in the days when the latter was in the habit of coming down like the wolf on the fold. *What?* Manship had been using no weapon of his own. He had, so far as he knew, no ally on this world. He looked about the huge, vaulted room. Silence. There was nothing else, nobody else in the place.

What was it the professor had screamed telepathically before he turned into soup? Something about Manship's eyes? Something *coming* out of the Earthman's eyes?

Still intensely puzzled—and despite his relief at having survived the last few minutes—Manship could not help regretting Lirld's extinction. Possibly because of his somewhat similar occupational status, the flefnobe had been the only creature of his type toward whom Manship felt any sympathy. He felt a little lonelier now—and, obscurely, a little guilty.

The different thoughts which had been mashing themselves to and fro in his mind abruptly disappeared, to be replaced by a highly important observation.

The zig-zag doorway through which Srin had fled was

118

closing, was coming together! And, as far as Manship knew, it was the only way out of the place!

Manship bounced off the huge table-top in a jump that for the second time in ten minutes did great credit to a few semester hours of gym some six years ago. He reached the narrowing gap, prepared to claw his way through the solid stone if necessary.

He was determined not to be trapped in this place when the flefnobe police closed in with whatever they used in place of tear gas and machine guns. He had also not forgotten the need to catch up to Rabd and get two or three more driving lessons.

To his intense relief, the aperture dilated again as he was about to hit it. Some sort of photoelectric gadget, he wondered, or was it just sensitive to the approach of a body?

He charged through, and for the first time found himself on the surface of the planet with the night sky all around him.

The view of the sky almost took his breath away and made him forget, temporarily, the utterly strange city of the flefnobes that stretched away in every direction.

There were so many stars! It was as if these stellar bodies were so much confectioner's sugar and someone had tossed a bagful at the heavens. They glowed with enough luminosity to maintain a three-quarters twilight. There was no moon, but its lack was not felt; rather it seemed that half a dozen moons had been broken up into quadrillions of tiny white dots.

It would be impossible, in this plenty, to trace out a single constellation. It would be necessary, instead, Manship guessed, to speak of a third brightest patch, a fifth largest sector. Truly, here in the center of the Galaxy, one did not merely see the stars—one lived amongst them!

He noticed his feet were wet. Glancing down, he saw he was standing in a very shallow stream of some reddish liquid that flowed between the rounded flefnobe buildings. Sewage disposal? Water supply? Probably neither, probably something else completely out of the range of human needs. For there were other colored streams flowing parallel to it, Manship saw now—green ones, mauve ones, bright pink ones. At a street intersection a few yards from him, the reddish stream flowed away by itself down a sort of alley, while a few new colored ribbons joined the main body.

Well, he wasn't here to work out problems in extraterrestrial sociology. He already had the sniffling intimation of a bad head cold. Not only his feet were wet in this spongelike atmosphere; his pajamas clung to his skin in dampest companionship and, every once in a while, his eyes got blurry with the moisture and he had to brush them dry with the back of a hand.

Furthermore, while he was not hungry, he had not only seen nothing resembling human-type victuals since his arrival, but also no evidence to suggest that the flefnobes had stomachs, let alone mouths.

Maybe they took in nourishment through the skin, soaked it up, say, from those differently colored streams that ran through their city. Red might be meat, green could be vegetables, while for dessert—

He clenched his fists and shook himself. *I've no time for any of this philosophic badminton*, he told himself fiercely. *In just a few hours, I'm going to be extremely hungry and thirsty. I'm also going to be extremely hunted. I'd better get moving—work out some solutions!*

Only where? Fortunately, the street outside Lirld's laboratory seemed deserted. Maybe the flefnobes were afraid of the dark? Maybe they were all good, respectable homebodies and everyone, without exception, toddled into his bed at night to sleep the darkness through? Maybe—

Rabd. He had to find Rabd. That was the beginning and the end of the only solution to his problems he had come even close to, since his materialization on Professor Lirld's lab table.

Rabd.

He tried "listening" with his mind. All kinds of drifting, miscellaneous thoughts were sloshing around in his brain, from the nearer inhabitants of the city.

"All right, darling, all right. If you don't want to *gadl*, you don't have to *gadl*. We'll do something else . . ."

"That smart-aleck Bohrg! Will I fix him properly tomorrow . . ."

120

"Do you have three *zamshkins* for a *plet?* I want to make a long-distance send . . ."

"Bohrg will roll in tomorrow morning, thinking everything is the same as it's always been. Is he going to be surprised . . ."

"I like you, Nernt, I like you a lot. And that's why I feel it's my duty to tell you, strictly as a friend, you understand . . ."

"No, darling, I didn't mean that *I* didn't want to *gadl*. I thought *you* didn't want to; I was trying to be considerate like you always tell me to be. *Of course* I want to *gadl*. Now please don't look at me like that . . ."

"Listen here. I can lick any flefnobe in the place . . ."

"To tell you the truth, Nernt, I think you're the only one who doesn't know. Everybody else . . ."

"So you're all scared, huh? All right, I'll take you on two at a time. Come on, *come on* . . ."

But no hint of Rabd. Manship began to walk cautiously down the stone-paved streets, sloshing through the little rivulets.

He stepped too close to the wall of the dark buildings. Immediately, a zig-zag doorway opened its jagged invitation. He hesitated for a moment, then stepped through.

Nobody here either. Did the flefnobes sleep in some central building, dormitory fashion? Did they sleep at all? He must remember to tune in on some likely mind and investigate. The information might be useful.

This building seemed to be a warehouse; it was filled with shelves. The walls were bare, however—there seemed to be some flefnobe inhibition against putting objects against the walls. The shelves rose in tall tiers—again free-form shapes—from the center of the floor.

Manship strolled over to the shelving that was the height of his chest. Dozens of fat green balls rested in white porcelain cups. Food? Could be. They looked distinctly edible, like melons.

He reached out and picked one up. It immediately spread wings and flew away to the ceiling. Every one of the other green balls, on all the shelves, spread a similar set of multiple, tiny wings and flew upward, like so many spherical birds whose nests have been disturbed. When they reached the domed ceiling, they seemed to disappear.

Manship backed out of the place hurriedly through the jagged aperture. He seemed to be setting off alarms wherever he went!

Once out in the street, he sensed a new feeling. There was a sensation of bubbling excitement everywhere, a tense waiting. Very few individual thoughts were coming through.

Suddenly the restlessness coalesced into an enormous mental shout that almost deafened him.

"Good evening!" it said. "Please stand by for an emergency news bulletin. This is Pukr, the son of Kimp, coming to you on a planet-wide, mind-to-mind hookup. Here is the latest on the flat-eyed monster:

"At forty-three *skims* past *bebblewort*, tonight, this creature was materialized by Professor Lirld from astronomical unit 649-301-3 as part of an experiment in one-way teleportation. Councilor Glomg was present as a witness to the experiment in the course of his official duties and, observing the aggressive way in which the monster comported itself, immediately warned Lirld of the dangers in letting it remain alive.

"Lirld disregarded the warning and, later, after Councilor Glomg had departed with his son, Rabd, the well-known interplanetary explorer and flefnobe-about-town, the monster ran amuck. Having fought its way out of a cage of solid paper, it attacked the professor with an unknown type of high-frequency mental beam that seems to emanate from its unbelievably flat eyes. This beam seems to be similar, in effect, to that thrown out by second-order *grepsas* when all fuses have blown. Our best psychophysicists are, at this very moment, working feverishly on that aspect of the problem.

"But Professor Lirld paid with his life for his scientific curiosity and for disregarding the warnings of Councilor Glomg's experience. Despite the best efforts of Srin, Lirld's laboratory assistant, who fought a desperate and courageous diversionary action in an attempt to save the old scientist, Lirld perished horribly before the monster's ferocious onslaught. With his superior dead, Srin retreated tentacle by tentacle, fighting all the way, barely managing to make his escape in time.

"This alien monster with its incredible powers is now loose in our city! All citizens are urged to remain calm, not to panic. Rest assured that as soon as the authorities know what to do, they will do it. Remember—above all—stay calm!

"Meanwhile, Rabd, the son of Glomg, has postponed his mating flight which was to have begun tonight. He is mating, as you all know, with Tekt, the daughter of Hilp —Tekt being the well-known star of *fnesh* and *blelg* from the southern continent. Rabd is leading a troop of volunteer flefnobes to the scientific quarters of the city, where the monster was last seen, in an attempt to exterminate it with already-existing, conventional weapons before the creature starts to reproduce. I will return with more bulletins when they are available. That is all for now."

That was more than enough, Manship felt. Now there wasn't any hope that he could work out some method of communication with these creatures and sit down for a little quiet conversation on ways and means of getting himself home—which seemed to be a conclusion earnestly desired by all. From now on the watchword was going to be *Get That Manship!*

He didn't like that at all.

On the other hand, he didn't have to wander after Rabd. If Manship can't get to the flefnobe, the flefnobe will come to Manship. Heavily armed, however, and with homicidal intent . . .

He decided he had better hide. He stepped up to a building and wandered along a wall until the doorway opened. He walked through and watched it close behind him, then looked around.

To his relief, it seemed like an excellent place to hide. There were quantities of large, heavy objects in the center of the place, none of them, so far as he could tell, alive, and all of them satisfactorily opaque. He wedged himself between two of these which looked like stored table-tops and hoped wistfully that the flefnobe sensory apparatus did not boast any more detective mechanisms than he had already experienced.

What he wouldn't give to be an assistant professor in Kelly University again instead of a flat-eyed monster ravening, all unwittingly, through an alien metropolis!

He found himself wondering about the strange powers he was supposed to possess. What was all this nonsense about a high-frequency mental beam emanating from his eyes? He hadn't noticed anything coming out—and he should have noticed if anyone did, he felt. Yet Lirld had made some comment to that effect just before he dissolved.

Was it possible that there was some by-product of the human brain that was only visible to flefnobes and was highly deleterious to them?

After all, he could tune in on the flefnobes' minds and they couldn't tune in on his. Maybe the only way he could make his mental presence felt to them was in some prodigious blast of thought which literally ripped them apart.

But he evidently couldn't turn it on and off at will—he hadn't caused the slightest alteration in Lirld, the first time the professor had fired.

There were ripples of new, excited thoughts reaching him suddenly. They were coming from somewhere in the street outside.

Rabd had arrived with his posse.

"Three of you move down that way," the young flefnobe ordered. "I want two each to cover the side streets. Don't spend too much time searching through the buildings. I'm positive we'll find this monster skulking somewhere in the dark streets, looking for new victims. Tanj, Zogt and Lewv—come with me. And keep on your tentacle-tips, everybody—this thing is crazy dangerous. But remember, we've got to blast it before it starts reproducing. Imagine what this planet would be like with a couple of hundred of these flat-eyed monsters running around!"

Manship let out a long, slow sigh of relief. If they hoped to find him on the streets, he might have a little time.

He let his mind follow that of Rabd. It wasn't too hard —just a matter of concentration—and you pretty much blocked out the thoughts of the other individuals. *Follow Rabd's mind. Rabd's thoughts. Now block out most of Rabd's conscious thoughts. There. The subliminal layer, the memory patterns. No, not the stuff about that female flefnobe last month, all eyes and soft tentacles, dammit!*

The memory patterns, the older ones. "When landing on a C-12 type planet . . ." *No, not that one. A little further. There!* "Having fired the forward jet to clear it, gently depress the . . ."

Manship combed through the operational instructions in Rabd's mind, pausing every once in a while to clear up a concept peculiar to flefnobe terminology, stopping now and then as a grinning thought about Tekt wandered in and threw everything out of focus.

He noticed that whatever information he absorbed in this fashion, he seemed to absorb permanently; there was no need to go back to previous data. Probably left a permanent print on his mind, he concluded.

He had it all now, at least as much about running the ship as it was possible to understand. In the last few moments, he had been operating the ship—and operating the ship for years and years—at least through Rabd's memories. For the first time, Manship began to feel a little confident.

But how was he to find the little spaceship in the streets of this utterly strange city? He clasped his hands in perspired bafflement. After all this—

Then he had the answer. He'd get the directions from Rabd's mind. Of course. Good old encyclopedia Rabd! *He'd* certainly remember where he parked the vessel.

And he did. With a skill that seemed to have come from ages of practice, Clyde Manship riffled through the flefnobe's thoughts, discarding this one, absorbing that one— ". . . the indigo stream for five blocks. Then take the first merging red one and . . ." —until he had as thorough and as permanent a picture of the route to Rabd's three-jet runabout as if he'd been studying the subject in graduate school for six months.

Pretty good going for a stodgy young assistant professor of Comparative Literature who up to this night had about as much experience with telepathy as African lion-hunting! But perhaps—perhaps it had been a matter of *conscious* experience of telepathy; perhaps the human mind was accustomed to a sort of regular, deep-in-the-brain, unconscious telepathy from infancy and being exposed to creatures so easy to receive from as flefnobes had brought the latently exercised powers to the surface.

That would explain the quickly acquired skill that felt so much like the sudden surprising ability to type whole words and sentences after months of practicing nothing but meaningless combinations of letters in certain set alphabetical patterns.

Well, it might be interesting, but that particular speculation was not his field of research and not his problem. Not for tonight, anyway.

Right now, what he had to do was somehow slip out of the building unobserved by the crowd of flefnobe vigilantes outside, and get on his way fast. After all, it might not be long before the militia was called out to deal with something as viciously destructive as himself. . . .

He slipped out of his hiding-place and made for the wall. The zig-zag doorway opened. He stepped through —and bowled over a tentacled black suitcase who'd apparently been coming in.

The flefnobe recovered fast. He pointed his spiraly weapon at Manship from where he lay and began winding it. Once more, the Earthman went rigid with fright; he'd seen what that thing could do. To be killed now, after all he'd gone through . . .

And once more, there was a quiver and a mental scream of distress from the flefnobe: "The flat-eyed monster— I've found him—his eyes—his eyes. Zogt, Rabd, help! *His eyes*—"

There was nothing left but a twitching tentacle or two and a puddle of liquid rippling back and forth in a little hollow near the building wall. Without looking back, Manship fled.

A stream of red dots chattered over his shoulder and dissolved a domed roof directly ahead of him. Then he had turned the corner and was picking up speed. From the dwindling telepathic shouts behind him, he deduced with relief that feet moved faster than tentacles.

He found the correct colored streams and began to work his way in the direction of Rabd's spaceship. Only once or twice did he come across a flefnobe. And none of them seemed to be armed.

At sight of him, these passersby wound their tentacles about their bodies, huddled against the nearest wall, and, after a few dismal mutters to the effect of "*Qrm* save me, *Qrm* save me," seemed to pass out.

He was grateful for the absence of heavy traffic, but wondered why it should be so, especially since he was now moving through the residential quarters of the city according to the mental map he had purloined from Rabd.

Another overpowering roar in his mind gave him the answer.

"This is Pukr, the son of Kimp, returning to you with more news of the flat-eyed monster. First, the Council wishes me to notify all who have not already been informed through their *blelg* service that a state of martial law has been proclaimed in the city.

"Repeat: a state of martial law has been proclaimed in the city! All citizens are to stay off the streets until further notice. Units of the army and space fleet as well as heavy *maizeltoovers* are being moved in hurriedly. Don't get in their way! Stay off the streets!

"The flat-eyed monster has struck again. Just ten short *skims* ago, it struck down Lewv, the son of Yifg, in a running battle outside the College of Advanced *Turkaslerg*, almost trampling Rabd, the son of Glomg, who courageously hurled himself in its path in a valiant attempt to delay the monster's flight. Rabd, however, believes he seriously wounded it with a well-placed bolt from his blaster. The monster's weapon was the high-frequency beam from its eyes—

"Shortly before this battle, the flat-eyed horror from the outer galactic wastes had evidently wandered into a museum where it completely destroyed a valuable collection of green *fermfnaks*. They were found in a useless winged condition. Why did it do this? Pure viciousness? Some scientists believe that this act indicates intelligence of a very high order indeed, and that this intelligence, together with the fantastic powers already in evidence,

127

will make the killing of the monster a much more difficult task than the local authorities expect.

"Professor Wuvb is one of these scientists. He feels that only through a correct psycho-sociological evaluation of the monster and an understanding of the peculiar cultural milieu from which it evidently derives will we be able to work out adequate counter-measures and save the planet. Therefore, in the interests of flefnobe survival, we have brought the professor here tonight to give you his views. The next mind you hear will be that of Professor Wuvb."

Just as the newcomer began portentously, "To understand any given cultural milieu, we must first ask ourselves what we mean by culture. Do we mean, for example —" Manship reached the landing field.

He came out upon it near the corner on which Rabd's three-jet runabout was parked between an enormous interplanetary vessel being loaded with freight and what Manship would have been certain was a warehouse, if he hadn't learned so thoroughly how wrong he could be about flefnobe equivalents of human activities.

There seemed to be no guards about, the landing field was not particularly well-lit, and most of the individuals in the neighborhood were concentrated around the freighter.

He took a deep breath and ran for the comparatively tiny, spherical ship with the deep hollow in the top and bottom, something like an oversized metallic apple. He reached it, ran around the side until he came to the zigzag line that indicated an entrance and squeezed through.

As far as he could tell, he hadn't been observed. Outside of the mutter of loading and stowage instructions coming from the larger ship, there were only Professor Wuvb's louder thoughts weaving their intricate socio-philosophical web: ". . . So we may conclude that in this respect, at least, the flat-eyed monster does not show the typical basic personality pattern of an illiterate. But then, if we attempt to relate the characteristics of a preliterate urban cultural configuration . . ."

Manship waited for the doorway to contract, then made his way hand over hand up a narrow, twisting ladderlike affair to the control room of the vessel. He seated himself

128

uncomfortably before the main instrument panel and went to work.

It was difficult using fingers on gadgets which had been designed for tentacles, but he had no choice. "*To warm up the motors of the* Bulvonn *Drive*—" Gently, very gently, he rotated the uppermost three cylinders a complete turn each. Then, when the rectangular plate on his left began to show an even succession of red and white stripes across its face, he pulled on the large black knob protruding from the floor. A yowling roar of jets started from outside. He worked almost without conscious effort, letting memory take over. It was as if Rabd himself were getting the spaceship into operation.

A few seconds later, he was off the planet and in deep space.

He switched to interstellar operation, set the directional indicator for astronomical unit 649-301-3—and sat back. There was nothing else for him to do until the time came for landing. He was a little apprehensive about that part, but things had gone so well up to this point that he felt quite the interstellar daredevil. "Old Rocketfingers Manship," he grinned to himself smugly.

According to Rabd's subliminal calculations, he should be arriving on Earth—given the maximum output of the *Bulvonn* Drive which he was using—in ten to twelve hours. He was going to be more than a bit hungry and thirsty, but—What a sensation he was going to make! Even more of a sensation than he had left behind him. The flat-eyed monster with a high-frequency mental beam coming out of its eyes. . . .

What *had* that been? All that had happened to him, each time a flefnobe dissolved before his stare, was a good deal of fear. He had been terribly frightened that he was going to be blasted into tiny pieces and had, somewhere in the process of being frightened, evidently been able to throw out something pretty tremendous—to judge from results.

Possibly the abnormally high secretion of adrenalin in the human system at moments of stress was basically inimical to flefnobe body structure. Or maybe there was an entirely mental reaction in Man's brain at such times whose emanations caused the flefnobes to literally fall apart. It made sense:

If he was so sensitive to their thoughts, they should be sensitive to him in some way. And obviously, when he was very much afraid, that sensitivity showed up with a vengeance.

He put his hands behind his head and glanced up to check his meters. Everything was working satisfactorily. The brown circles were expanding and contracting on the *sekkel* board, as Rabd's mind had said they should; the little serrations on the edge of the control panel were moving along at a uniform rate, the visiscreen showed—*the visiscreen!*

Manship leaped to his feet. The visiscreen showed what seemed to be every vessel in the flefnobe army and space fleet—not to mention the heavy *maizeltoovers*—in hot pursuit of him. And getting closer.

There was one large spacecraft that had almost caught up and was beginning to exude a series of bright rays that, Manship remembered from Rabd's recollections, were grapples.

What could have caused all this commotion—the theft of a single jet runabout? The fear that he might steal the secrets of flefnobe science? They should have been so glad to get rid of him, especially before he started reproducing hundreds of himself all over the planet!

And then a persistent thought ripple from inside his own ship—a thought ripple which he had been disregarding all the time he had been concentrating on the unfamiliar problems of deep-space navigation—gave him a clue.

He had taken off with someone—or something—else in the ship!

Clyde Manship scurried down the twisting ladder to the main cabin. As he approached, the thoughts became clearer and he realized, even before the cabin aperture dilated to let him through, exactly whom he would find.

Tekt.

The well-known female star of *fnesh* and *blelg* from the southern continent and Rabd's about-to-be bride cowered in a far corner; all of her tentacles—including the hundred and seventy-six slime-washed ones that were topped by

130

limpid eyes—twisted about her tiny black body in the most complicated series of knots Manship had ever seen.

"Oo-ooh!" her mind moaned. "*Qrm! Qrm!* Now it's going to happen! That awful, horrible thing! It's going to happen to me! It's coming closer—closer—"

"Look, lady, I'm not even slightly interested in you," Manship began, before he remembered that he'd never been able to communicate with any flefnobe before, let alone a hysterical female one.

He felt the ship shudder as the grapples touched it. *Well, here I go again,* he thought. In a moment there would be boarders and he'd have to turn them into bluish soup.

Evidently, Tekt had been sleeping aboard the vessel when he took off. She'd been waiting for Rabd to return and begin their mating flight. And she was obviously a sufficiently important figure to have every last reserve called up.

His mind caught the sensation of someone entering the ship. Rabd. From what Manship could tell, he was alone, carrying his trusty blaster—and determined to die fighting.

Well, that's exactly what he'd have to do. Clyde Manship was a fairly considerate individual and heartily disliked the idea of disintegrating a bridegroom on what was to have been his honeymoon. But, since he had found no way of communicating his pacific intentions, he had no choice.

"Tekt!" Rabd telepathed softly. "Are you all right?"

"Murder!" Tekt screamed. "Help-help-help-help . . ." Her thoughts abruptly disappeared; she had fainted.

The zig-zag aperture widened and Rabd bounced into the cabin, looking like a series of long balloons in his spacesuit. He glanced at the recumbent Tekt and then turned desperately, pointing his curlicued blaster at Manship.

"Poor guy," Manship was thinking. "Poor, dumb, narrow-minded hero type. In just a second, you'll be nothing but goo." He waited, full of confidence.

He was so full of confidence, in fact, that he wasn't a bit frightened.

So nothing came out of his eyes, nothing but a certain condescending sympathy.

So Rabd blasted the ugly, obscene, horrible, flat-eyed thing down where it stood. And scooped up his bride with loving tentacles. And went back home to a hero's reception.

THE HUMAN ANGLE

WHAT A ROAD! What filthy, dismal, blinding rain! And, by the ghost of old Horace Greeley, what an idiotic, impossible assignment!

John Shellinger cursed the steamy windshield from which a monotonous wiper flipped raindrops. He stared through the dripping, half-clear triangle of glass and tried to guess which was broken country road and which was the overgrown brown vegetation of autumn. He might have passed the slowly moving line of murderous men stretching to right and left across country and road; he might have angled off into a side-road and be heading off into completely forsaken land. But he didn't think he had.

What an assignment!

"Get the human angle on this vampire hunt," Randall had ordered. "All the other news services will be giving it the hill-billy twist, medieval superstition messing up the atomic world. What dumb jerks these dumb jerks are! You stay off that line. Find yourself a weepy individual slant on bloodsucking and sob me about three thousand words. And keep your expense account down—you just can't work a big swindle sheet out of that kind of agricultural slum."

So I saddles my convertible, Shellinger thought morosely, and I tools off to the pappy-mammy country where nobody speaks to strangers nohow "specially now, 'cause the vampire done got to three young 'uns already." And nobody will tell me the names of those three kids or whether any of them are still alive; and Randall's wires keep asking when I'll start sending usable copy; and I still can't find one loquacious Louise in the whole country. Wouldn't even have known of this cross-country hunt if I hadn't begun to wonder where all the men in town had disappeared to on such an unappetizing, rainy evening.

The road was bad in second, but it was impossible in almost any other gear. The ruts weren't doing the springs any good, either. Shellinger rubbed moisture off the glass with his handkerchief and wished he had another pair of headlights. He could hardly see.

That dark patch ahead, for instance. Might be one of the vampire posse. Might be some beast driven out of cover by the brush-beating. Might even be a little girl.

He ground into his brake. It was a girl. A little girl with dark hair and blue jeans. He twirled the crank and stuck his head out into the falling rain.

"Hey, kid. Want a lift?"

The child stooped slightly against the somber background of night and decaying, damp countryside. Her eyes scanned the car, came back to his face and considered it. The kid had probably not known that this chromium-plated kind of post-war auto existed. She'd certainly never dreamed of riding in one. It would give her a chance to crow over the other kids in the 'tater patch.

Evidently deciding that he wasn't the kind of stranger her mother had warned her about and that it would be less uncomfortable in the car than walking in the rain and mud, she nodded. Very slowly, she came around the front and climbed in at his right.

"Thanks, mister," she said.

Shellinger started again and took a quick, sidewise glance at the girl. Her blue jeans were raggedy and wet. She must be terribly cold and uncomfortable, but she wasn't going to let him know. She would bear up under it with the stoicism of the hill people.

But she was frightened. She sat hunched up, her hands folded neatly in her lap, at the far side of the seat right up against the door. What was the kid afraid of? Of course, the vampire!

"How far up do you go?" he asked her gently.

133

" 'Bout a mile and a half. But that way." She pointed over her shoulder with a pudgy thumb. She was plump, much more flesh on her than most of these scrawny, sharecropper kids. She'd be beautiful, too, some day, if some illiterate lummox didn't cart her off to matrimony and hard work in a drafty cabin.

Regretfully, he maneuvered around on the road, got the car turned and started back. He'd miss the hunters, but you couldn't drag an impressionable child into that sort of grim nonsense. He might as well take her home first. Besides, he wouldn't get anything out of those uncommunicative farmers with their sharpened stakes and silver bullets in their squirrel rifles.

"What kind of crops do your folks raise—tobacco or cotton?"

"They don't raise nothing yet. We just came here."

"Oh." That was all right: she didn't have a mountain accent. Come to think of it, she was a little more dignified than most of the children he'd met in this neighborhood. "Isn't it a little late to go for a stroll? Aren't your folks afraid to let you out this late with a vampire around?"

She shivered. "I—I'm careful," she said at last.

Hey! Shellinger thought. Here was the human angle. Here was what Randall was bleating about. A frightened little girl with enough curiosity to swallow her big lump of fear and go out exploring on this night of all others. He didn't know how it fitted, just yet—but his journalistic nose was twitching. There was copy here; the basic, colorful human angle was sitting fearfully on his red leather seat.

"Do you know what a vampire is?"

She looked at him, startled, dropped her eyes and studied her folded hands for words. "It's—it's like someone who needs people instead of meals." A hesitant pause. "Isn't it?"

"Ye-es." That was good. Trust a child to give you a fresh viewpoint, unspoiled by textbook superstition. He'd use that—"People instead of meals." "A vampire is supposed to be a person who will be immortal—not die, that is—so long as he or she gets blood and life from living people. The only way you can kill a vampire—"

"You turn right here, mister."

He pointed the car into the little branchlet of side road. It was annoyingly narrow; surprised wet boughs tapped the windshield, ran their leaves lazily across the car's fabric top. Once in a while, a tree top sneezed collected rain water down.

Shellinger pressed his face close to the windshield and tried to decipher the picture of brown mud amid weeds that his headlights gave him. "What a road! Your folks are really starting from scratch. Well, the only way to kill a vampire is with a silver bullet. Or you can drive a stake through the heart and bury it in a crossroads at midnight. That's what those men are going to do tonight if they catch it." He turned his head as he heard her gasp. "What's the matter—don't you like the idea?"

"I think it's horrid," she told him emphatically.

"Why? How do you feel—live and let live?"

She thought it over, nodded, smiled. "Yes, live and let live. Live and let live. After all—" She was having difficulty finding the right words again. "After all, some people can't help what they are. I mean," very slowly, very thoughtfully, "like if a person's a vampire, what can they do about it?"

"You've got a good point there, kid." He went back to studying what there was of the road. "The only trouble's this: if you believe in things like vampires, well, you don't believe in them good—you believe in them nasty. Those people back in the village who claim three children have been killed or whatever it was by the vampire, they hate it and want to destroy it. If there are such things as vampires—mind you, I said 'if'—then, by nature, they do such horrible things that any way of getting rid of them is right. See?"

"No. You shouldn't drive stakes through people."

Shellinger laughed. "I'll say you shouldn't. Never could like that deal myself. However, if it were a matter of a vampire to me or mine, I think I could overcome my squeamishness long enough to do a little roustabout work on the stroke of twelve."

He paused and considered that this child was a little

too intelligent for her environment. She didn't seem to be bollixed with superstitions as yet, and he was feeding her *Shellinger on Black Magic.* That was vicious. He continued, soberly, "The difficulty with those beliefs is that a bunch of grown men who hold them are spread across the countryside tonight because they think a vampire is on the loose. And they're likely to flush some poor hobo and finish him off gruesomely for no other reason than that he can't give a satisfactory explanation for his presence in the fields on a night like this."

Silence. She was considering his statement. Shellinger liked her dignified thoughtful attitude. She was a bit more at ease, he noticed, and was sitting closer to him. Funny how a kid could sense that you wouldn't do her any harm. Even a country kid. Especially a country kid, come to think of it, because they lived closer to nature or something.

He had won her confidence, though, and consequently rewon his. A week of living among thin-lipped ignoramuses who had been not at all diffident in showing *their* disdain had made him a little uncertain. This was better. And he'd finally got a line on the basis of a story.

Only, he'd have to dress it up. In the story, she'd be an ordinary hill-billy kid, much thinner, much more unapproachable; and the quotes would all be in "mountain" dialect.

Yes, he had the human interest stuff now.

She had moved closer to him again, right against his side. Poor kid! His body warmth made the wet coldness of her jeans a little less uncomfortable. He wished he had a heater in the car.

The road disappeared entirely into tangled bushes and gnarly trees. He stopped the car, flipped the emergency back.

"You don't live here? This place looks as if nothing human's been around for years."

He was astonished at the uncultivated desolation.

"Sure I live here, mister," her warm voice said at his ear. "I live in that little house over there."

"Where?" He rubbed at the windshield and strained

his vision over the sweep of headlight. "I don't see any house. Where is it?"

"There." A plump hand came up and waved at the night ahead. "Over there."

"I still can't see—" The corner of his right eye had casually noticed that the palm of her hand was covered with fine brown hair.

Strange, that.

Was covered with fine brown hair. Her palm!

"What *was* that you remembered about the shape of her teeth?" his mind shrieked. He started to whip his head around, to get another look at her teeth. But he couldn't.

Because her teeth were in his throat.

A MAN OF FAMILY

STEWART RALEY found his seat in the Commuter's Special —the stratojet that carried him every day from the Metropolitan New York Business Area to his suburban home in northern New Hampshire—with legs that literally felt not and eyes that really and truly saw not.

It was pure habit, years and years of the same repetitive act, that enabled him to find his accustomed place at the window beside Ed Greene; it was habit that pushed his forefinger at the button imbedded in the seat back immediately ahead of him; and it was habit that then kept him staring at the late-afternoon news telecast in the tiny seat-back screen, even though none of his senses registered a single one of the rapid-fire, excitedly announced bulletins.

He did hear, dimly, the scream of the jet's takeoff, but it was habit again that kept his feet firm on the floor and that tensed his abdominal muscles against the encircling safety belt. And that meant, he realized, that he was getting closer to a situation where habit would be of no help at all—

where nothing would be of any help. Not against about the worst possible thing that could happen to a man in 2080 A.D.

"Had a rough day, Stew?" Ed Greene asked him with beery loudness. "You look tired as hell."

Raley felt his lips move, but it was a while before sound came out of his throat. "Yes," he said finally. "I had a rough day."

"Well, and who asked you to work for Solar Minerals?" Ed asked, as if he were replying to a sharply phrased argument. "These interplanetary corporations are all the same: pressure, pressure, pressure. You got to get the invoices ready right now, this minute, this second, because the Neptunian supply ship is leaving and there won't be another one for six months; you got to get the Mercury correspondence all dictated because— Don't I know? I worked for Outer Planet Pharmaceuticals fifteen years ago and I had a goddam bellyful. Give me the real-estate racket and accounts in the Metropolitan New York Business Area. Quiet. Solid. Calm."

Raley nodded heavily and rubbed at his forehead. He didn't have a headache, but he wished he had one. He wished he had anything that would make it impossible for him to think.

"Course, there's not much money in it," Ed went on, boomingly viewing the other side of the question. "There's not much money, but there's no ulcers either. I'll probably be stuck in a two-child bracket all my life— but it'll be a long life. We take things slow and easy in my office. We know little old New York's been here a long time, and it'll be here a long time to come."

"Yes," Raley said, still staring straight ahead of him. "It will be. New York will be here for a long time to come."

"Well, don't say it in such a miserable tone of voice, man! Ganymede will be here for a long time, too! No one's going to run away with Ganymede!"

Frank Tyler leaned forward from behind them. "How about a little seven-card stud, fellas?" he inquired. "We've got a half-hour to kill."

Raley didn't feel at all like playing cards, but he felt too grateful to Frank to refuse. His fellow-employee at Solar

Minerals had been listening to Greene—as, inevitably, had everyone else on the plane—and he alone knew what anguish the real-estate man had been unconsciously creating. He'd probably got more and more uncomfortable and had decided to provide a distraction, any distraction.

Nice of him, Raley thought, as he and Ed spun their seats around so that they faced the other way. After all, he'd been promoted to the Ganymede desk over Frank's head; another man in Frank's position might have enjoyed hearing Ed sock it to him. Not Frank, he was no ghoul.

It was the usual game, with the usual four players. Bruce Robertson, the book illustrator, who sat on Frank Tyler's left, brought his huge portfolio up off the floor and placed it table-wise on their knees. Frank opened a fresh deck and they cut for deal. Ed Greene won.

"Usual stakes?" he asked, as he shuffled the cards. "Ten, twenty, thirty?"

They nodded, and Ed began to lay out a hand. He didn't stop talking though.

"I was telling Stew," he explained in a voice that must have carried clear to the pilot in his sealed-off cabin, "that real estate is good for the blood pressure, if not much else. My wife is all the time telling me to move into a more hotshot field. 'I feel so ashamed,' she says, 'a woman of my age with only two children. Stewart Raley is ten years younger than you and already Marian has had her fourth baby. If you were half a man, you'd be ashamed, too. If you were half a man, you'd *do* something about it.' You know what I tell her? 'Sheila,' I say, 'the trouble with you is you're 36A-happy.'"

Bruce Robertson looked up, puzzled. "36A?"

Ed Greene guffawed. "Oh, you lucky bachelor, you! Wait'll you get married! You'll find out what 36A is all right. You'll eat, sleep and drink 36A."

"Form 36A," Frank Tyler explained to Bruce quietly as he raked in the pot, "is what you fill out when you make application to the FPB for permission to have another child."

"Oh. Of course. I just didn't know the number. But wait a minute, Ed. Economic status is only one of the

139

factors. The Family Planning Bureau also considers health of the parents, heredity, home environment—"

"What did I tell you?" Ed crowed. "A bachelor! A wet-behind-the-ears, no-child bachelor!"

Bruce Robertson turned white. "I'll be getting married one of these days, Ed Greene," he said through tightly set teeth. "And when I do, I'll have more children than you ever—"

"You're right about economic status being only one of the factors," Frank Tyler broke in hurriedly, peaceably. "But it's the most important single factor, and if there already are a couple of children in the family, and they seem to be in pretty good shape, it's the factor that the FPB considers to the exclusion of almost everything else in handing down its decision."

"Right!" Ed brought his hand down positively and the cards danced about on the portfolio-table. "Take my brother-in-law, Paul. Day and night, my wife is going *Paul this, Paul that*; it's no wonder I know more about him than I do myself. Paul owns half of Mars-Earth Freighting Syndicate, so he's in an eighteen-child bracket. His wife's sort of lazy, she doesn't care much for appearances, so they only have ten children, but—"

"Do they live in New Hampshire?" Frank asked. A moment before, Stewart Raley had noticed Frank glancing at him with real concern: he was evidently trying to change the subject, feeling that the direction the conversation had taken could only make Raley more miserable. It probably showed on his face.

He'd have to do something about his face: he'd be meeting Marian in a few minutes. If he wasn't careful, she'd guess immediately.

"New Hampshire?" Ed demanded contemptuously. "My brother-in-law, Paul? With *his* money? No, sir! No backyard suburb for him! He lives in the *real* country, west of Hudson Bay, up in Canada. But, like I was saying, he and his wife don't get along so good, the home life for the kids isn't the best in the world, if you know what I mean. You think they have trouble getting a 36A okayed? Not on your life! They fill it out and it's back the next morning with a big blue *approved* all over it. The way

140

the FPB figures, what the hell, with their money they can afford to hire first-class nursemaids and child psychologists, and if the kids still have trouble when they grow up, they'll get the best mental therapy that money can buy."

Bruce Robertson shook his head. "That doesn't sound right to me. After all, prospective parents are being turned down every day for negative heredity."

"Heredity is one thing," Ed pointed out. "Environment's another. One can't be changed—the other can. And let me tell you, mister, the thing that makes the biggest change in the environment is money. M-O-N-E-Y: money, cash, gelt, moolah, wampum, the old spondulix. Enough money, and, the FPB figures your kid *has* to have a good start in life—especially with it supervising the early years. Your deal Stew. Hey, Stew! You in mourning for that last pot? You haven't said a word for the past fifteen minutes. Anything wrong? You didn't get fired today, did you?"

Raley tried to pull himself together. He picked up the cards. "No," he said thickly. "I didn't get fired."

Marian was waiting with the family jetabout at the landing field. Fortunately, she was too full of gossip to be very observant. She looked oddly at him only once, when he kissed her.

"That was a poor, tired thing," she said. "You used to do a lot better than that."

He dug his fingernails into his palms and tried to be whimsical. "That was before I was a poor, tired thing. Had a real hard day at the office. Be sweet and gentle with me, honey, and don't expect too much."

She nodded sympathetically and they climbed into the small craft. Lisa, twelve years old and their first child, was in the back seat with Mike, the latest. Lisa kissed her father resoundingly and then held up the baby for a similar ceremony.

He found he had to force himself to kiss the baby.

They shot up into the air. All around them, the jetabouts radiated away from the landing field. Stewart Raley stared at the suburban roofs rushing by below and tried to decide when he was going to tell her. After supper, that would be a good time. No, better wait until the children were all in bed. Then, when he and Marian were alone in the living room—

He felt his stomach go solid and cold, just as it had that afternoon after lunch. Would he be able to bring himself to tell her at all, he wondered?

He had to. That was all there was to it. He had to—and tonight.

"—if I ever believed a word Sheila said in the first place," Marian was saying. "I told her: 'Connie Tyler is not that sort of woman, and that's enough for me.' You remember, darling, last month when Connie came to visit me in the hospital? Well, of course, I knew what she was thinking. She was looking at Mike and saying to herself that if Frank had only become head of the Ganymede department and had a two-thousand territ raise instead of you, *she'd* be having her fourth child now and I'd be visiting *her*. I knew what she was thinking, because in her place I'd be thinking exactly the same thing. But when she said it was the cutest, healthiest baby she'd ever seen, she was sincere. And when she wished me a fifth child for next year, she wasn't just being polite: she really meant it!"

A *fifth* child, Stewart Raley thought bitterly. A *fifth!*

"—so I leave it up to you. What should I do about Sheila if she comes around tomorrow and starts in all over again?"

"Sheila?" he asked stupidly. "Sheila?"

Marian shook her head impatiently over the controls. "Sheila Greene. Ed's wife, remember? Stewart, haven't you heard a word I said?"

"Sure, honey. About—uh, the hospital and Connie. And Mike. I heard everything you said. But where does Sheila come in?"

She turned around now and stared at him. The large green cat's-eyes, that had once pulled him across a dance floor to the side of a girl he didn't know, were very intent. Then she flipped a switch, letting the automatic pilot take over to keep them on course. "Something's wrong, Stewart. And it's not just a hard day at the office. Something's really wrong. What is it?"

"Later," he said. "I'll tell you later."

"No, now. Tell me now. I couldn't go through another second with you looking like that."

He blew out a chestful of breath and kept his eyes on the house-after-house-after-house beneath him.

"Jovian Chemicals bought the Keohula Mine today."

"So. What is that to you?"

"The Keohula Mine," he explained painfully, "is the only mine on Ganymede in full operation."

"I still—I'm afraid I still don't understand. Stewart, please tell me in words of one syllable, but tell me fast. What *is* it?"

He looked up, noticing how terrified she was. She had no idea what he was talking about, but she had always had remarkable instincts. Almost telepathic.

"With the Keohula Mine sold, and for a good price, Solar Minerals feels it is uneconomic to maintain an installation on Ganymede. There are therefore shutting it down, effective immediately."

Marian raised her hands to her mouth in horror. "And that means—that means—"

"That means they no longer need a Ganymede Department. Or a Ganymede Department Chief."

"But they won't send you back to your old job!" she cried. "That would be too cruel! They couldn't demote you, Stewart, not after you've gone and had another child on the strength of your raise! There must be another department, there must be—"

"There isn't," he told her with a tongue that felt like cardboard. "They're shutting down operations on all the Jovian satellites. I'm not the only one affected. There's Cartwright of the Europa desk and McKenzie of Io— they both have seniority over me. From now on, Solar Minerals is going to lean heavily on its holdings on Uranus, Neptune and Pluto, and light everywhere else."

"Well, what about *those* planets? They'll need department heads at Solar Minerals, won't they?"

Raley sighed helplessly. "They have them. *And* assistant department heads. Good men who know their work, who've handled it for years. And as far as your next question goes, honey, I've spoken to Jovian Chemicals

143

about a transfer. No go. They already have a Ganymede Department and the man handling it is very satisfactory. All day I kept trying one angle after another. But tomorrow, I'll be back in Ore Shipments."

"At your old salary?" she whispered. "Seven thousand territs a year?"

"Yes. Two thousand less than I'm getting now. Two thousand less than the minimum for four children."

Marian's hands crept up to her eyes, which filled, abruptly, with tears. "I'm not going to do it!" she sobbed. "I'm not! I'm not!"

"Honey," he said. "Honey-baby, it's the law. What can we do?"

"I absolutely—I absolutely refuse to decide which—which one of my children I'm going to—to give up!"

"I'll get promoted again. I'll be making nine thousand territs in no time. More, even. You'll see."

She stopped crying and stared at him dully. "But once a child is put up for adoption, the parents can't reclaim it. Even if their income increases. You know that, Stewart, as well as I. They can have other children, but they can't ever have the superfluous child back."

Of course he knew that. That regulation had been framed by the FPB to protect the foster-parents and encourage adoption into higher-bracket families. "We should have waited," he said. "Damn it, we should have waited!"

"We did," she reminded him. "We waited six months, to make certain your job was secure. Don't you remember the night that we had Mr. Halsey to dinner and he told us that you were working out very well and were definitely on your way up in the organization? 'You'll have ten children yet, Mrs. Raley,' he said, 'and my advice is to get started on them as soon as possible.' Those were his exact words."

"Poor Halsey. He couldn't meet my eyes all through the executive conference this afternoon. Just before I left the office, he came up and told me how sorry he was, how he'd look out for me in the very next promotion list. But he pointed out that practically everybody's retrenching these days; it's been a bad year for extra-terrestrial products. And when I move back into my old job in Ore Shipments, I bump back the man who took my place. He moves down and bumps back somebody else. It's hell all around."

Marian dried her eyes with determined waves of the dashboard breezespout. "*Our* problem's enough for me, Stewart. I'm not interested in anybody else right now. What can we do?"

He leaned back and grimaced. "The best I could think of—I called my lawyer. Cleve said he'd be down this evening after dinner to go over the whole matter with us. If there's an out, Cleve will find it. He's handled a lot of FPB appeals."

She inclined her head in recognition of this effort. "That's a beginning. How much time do we have?"

"Well, I have to file a Notice of Superfluity form tomorrow morning. We have two weeks to decide which—which child."

Marian nodded again. They sat there, letting the automatic pilot throb the jetabout to its destination. After a while, Stewart Raley reached across the seat and took his wife's hand. Her fingers curled about his fingers spasmodically.

"I know which child," said a voice from behind them.

They both turned around sharply. "Lisa!" Marian gasped. "I forgot you were here! You've been listening!"

Lisa's round cheeks were glistening with wetness. "I've been listening," she admitted. "And I know which child it has to be. Me. I'm the oldest. I'm the one who should be put up for adoption. Not Penny or Susie or Mike, but me."

"Now you shush up, Lisa Raley. Your father and I will decide what to do. It's more than possible that nothing will happen. Nothing at all."

"I'm the oldest, so I should be put up for adoption. That's what my teacher says is supposed to happen. My teacher says that the young children are af-affected more than older children. And my teacher says that it's a very good thing, because you're sure to be adopted by a very rich family and you get more toys and better schools and —and all sorts of things. My teacher says that maybe
145

you're a little s-sad at first, but you have so many good things happening to you, that—that you get to be very ha-happy. And anyway, my teacher says, that's the way it has to be, 'cause that's the law."

Stewart Raley hit the seat hard. "That's enough! Your mother said she and I will decide."

"And besides," Lisa went on defiantly, wiping her face with one hand, "besides, I don't *want* to be a member of a three-child family. All my friends are four-child family girls. I'd have to go back to those poky old friends I used to have, and I—"

"Lisa!" Raley roared. "I'm still your father! Do you want me to prove it to you?"

Silence. Marian switched back to manual for the landing. She took the baby from the twelve-year-old and they all got out of the jetabout without looking at each other.

Raley took a moment before entering the house to adjust the handi-robot from "Gardening" to "Waiting on Tables." Then he followed the whirring metal figure through the door.

The trouble was that Lisa was right. All other things being equal, the oldest child was the usual choice for outside adoption. For her, it was a much less traumatic experience. And the Family Planning Bureau would select the new parents carefully, from among the horde of applicants, and see to it that the transfer was made as smoothly and happily as possible. Child psychologists would make twice-weekly visits for the first few years, insuring the maximum adjustment to the new situation.

Who would the new parents be? Probably someone like Ed Greene's brother-in-law, Paul, someone whose income had far outstripped the permissible family. That could be due to a variety of reasons: a lazy, unconventional wife, latent sterility in either partner to the marriage, a suddenly necessary hysterectomy. In any case, something that left them without the means of achieving the only kind of prestige that mattered.

You could have a real flossy jetabout—but you might have bought it on credit and still owe ten years' worth of salary on it. You might have an enormous home in expensive, estate-filled Manitoba, where the top executives of the New York Business Area lived side by side with their opposite numbers from the Chicago and Los Angeles Business Areas, a home whose walls were paneled in rare Martian woods and which was replete with every kind of specialized robot—but, for all anyone knew, you might be doing it by carrying a mortgage which was slowly but surely choking you into financial submission.

Children, now, children were definite. You couldn't have a child on credit, you didn't have a child because you were expecting business to get better. You only had a child when the FPB, having accepted you and your wife heredity-wise and environment-wise, decided your income was large enough to give that child all the advantages it deserved. Every child a family had represented a license that the FPB issued only after the most searching investigation. And *that* was status.

That was why you didn't have to give job data or references when you were buying something on time if you could pull out a six-child license. The clerk just took down your name and address and the serial number on the license—and that was that. You walked out of the store with the merchandise.

All through supper, Raley thought about that. He couldn't help feeling doubly guilty over his demotion in Solar Minerals when he remembered what his first thought was on the morning the license to have Mike arrived. It was a jubilant *now we get into the country club, now they'll invite us to join.* He'd been happy about the permission to have another baby, of course—he and Marian both loved kids, and in quantity—but he'd already had three by then; it was the fourth child which was the big jump.

"Well," he said to himself, "and which father wouldn't have felt the same way? Even Marian, the day after Mike's birth, began calling him 'our country-club son.'"

Those were happy, pride-filled days. They'd walked the Earth, Marian and he, like young monarchs on their way to coronation. Now—

Cleveland Boettiger, Raley's lawyer, arrived just as Marian was scolding Lisa into bed. The two men went into the living room and had the handi-robot mix them a drink.

"I won't sugar-coat it, Stew," the lawyer said, spreading the contents of his briefcase on the antique coffee-table that Marian had cleverly converted from an early twentieth-century army foot-locker. "It doesn't look good. I've been going over the latest FPB rulings and, in terms of your situation, it doesn't look good."

"Isn't there any chance? Any angle?"

"Well, that's what we'll try to find tonight."

Marian came in and curled up on the sofa next to her husband. "That Lisa!" she exclaimed. "I almost had to spank her. She's already beginning to look on me as a stranger with no authority over her. It's maddening."

"Lisa insists that she's the one who should be put up for adoption," Raley explained. "She heard us talking about it."

Boettiger picked up a sheet covered with notes and shook it out. "Lisa's right, of course. She's the oldest. Now, let's review the situation. You two married on a salary of three thousand territs a year, the minimum for one child. That's Lisa. Three years later, accumulated raises brought your income up two thousand. That's Penelope. Another year and a half, another two thousand. Susan. Last year, in February, you took over the Ganymede desk at nine thousand a year. Mike. Today, you were demoted and went back to seven thousand, which is a maximum three-child bracket. Does that cover it?"

"That covers it," his host told him. *The story of my adult life*, he thought: *in a couple of sentences. It doesn't cover the miscarriage Marian almost had with Penny or the time the handi-robot short-circuited near the play-pen and we had to take six stitches in Susie's head. It doesn't cover the time—*

"All right, then, Stew, let's hit the income possibilities first. Do either of you have any hope of a sizable amount of money coming in soon, a legacy, say, or some piece of property that may substantially increase in value?"

They looked at each other. "Both Stewart's family and mine," Marian answered slowly, "are three- or four-child bracket people. There won't be much of an estate. And

148

all we own, besides the house and the furniture and the jetabout, are some government bonds and a little Solar Minerals stock that won't be worth much more than we paid for it for a long, long time."

"That takes care of income. Let me ask you people this, then—"

"Wait a minute," Raley burst out. "Why does it take care of income? Suppose I get a part-time job, working week-ends or evenings here in New Hampshire?"

"Because the license to have a child is predicated on the income from a normal thirty-hour week," the lawyer pointed out patiently. "If the father has to work additional time in order to reach or maintain that income, his child sees that much less of him and, in the legal phrase, 'is denied the normal prerogatives of a normal infancy.' Remember, the rights of the child are absolutely paramount in present-day law. There's no way around it."

Stewart Raley stared at the opposite wall. "We could emigrate," he said in a low voice. "There are no birth-control regulations on Venus or any of the other colonies."

"You're thirty-eight, Marian is thirty-two. They like 'em young, real young, on Mars and Venus—not to mention the fact that you're an office worker, not a technician or a mechanic or farmer. I doubt very much that you could get a permanent extra-terrestrial visa. No, the income possibilities are out. That leaves Special Hardship. Is there any claim you could think of under that heading?"

Marian saw a straw and clutched at it. "There might be something. I had to have a Caesarean when Mike was born."

"Um." Cleveland Boettiger reached for another document and studied it. "According to your medical data sheet, that was because of the child's position in the womb at birth. It is not expected to interfere in any way with future child-bearing. Anything else? Any negative psychological reports on Lisa, for example, that would make it inadvisable for her to transfer to another set of parents at this time? Think."

They thought. They sighed. There was nothing.

149

"Pretty much as I thought, then, Stew. It definitely doesn't look good. Well, suppose you sign this and hand it in with the Notice of Superfluity tomorrow. I've filled it out."

"What is it?" Marian asked, peering anxiously at the paper he had handed them.

"A Request for a Delay in Execution. The grounds I've given are that you were eminently satisfactory in your job and that therefore the demotion may be only temporary. It won't stand up once the FPB sends an investigator to your main office, but that will take time. You'll get an extra month to decide which child and—who knows?—maybe something will turn up by then. A better job with another outfit, another promotion."

"I couldn't get a better job with another outfit these days," Raley said miserably. "I'm lucky to have the one I do, the way things are. And a promotion is out for at least a year."

There was a screech outside as a jetabout landed on their lawn.

"Company?" Marian wondered. "We weren't expecting anyone."

Her husband shook his head. "*Company!* The last thing in the world we want tonight is company. See who it is, Marian, and tell them please to go away."

She left the living room, waving to the handi-robot, as she went, to refill Boettiger's empty glass. Her face was stiff with pain.

"I don't see," Stewart Raley exclaimed, "why the FPB has to be that rigid and meticulous in interpreting the birth-control statutes! Can't they give a guy a little leeway?"

"They do," the lawyer reminded him as he put the papers carefully back in the briefcase. "They certainly do. After the child has been approved and conceived, you're allowed a drop in income up to nine hundred territs—a concession to the unexpected. But two thousand, a whole two thousand . . ."

"It's unfair, though, it's damned unfair! After you have a child and raise it, for it to be taken away by a minor bureau of the world government is—"

"Now, Raley, don't be an ass!" Boettiger said sharply. "I'm your lawyer and I'll help you to the limits of my professional competence, but I won't sit here listening to you make noises that I know you don't believe yourself. Either family planning on a world-wide basis makes sense, or it doesn't. Either we make sure that each and every child is a wanted child, a valued child, with a solid chance for a decent, happy, fulfilled life, or we go back to the irresponsible, catch-as-catch-can childbearing methods of the previous centuries. We both know that intelligent family planning has made the world a far better place. Well, Form 36A is the symbol of family planning—and the Notice of Superfluity is just the reverse side of the coin. You cannot reasonably have one without the other."

Raley bowed his head and spread his hands. "I don't argue with that, Cleve. It's just—it's just—"

"It's just that the shoe happens to pinch you right now. I'm sorry for that, deeply sorry. But the way I feel is this: If a client comes to me and tells me he absent-mindedly flew his jetabout over a restricted area, I'll use all my legal education and every inch of my dirty mind to get him off with as low a fine as possible. When he goes further, though, and starts telling me that the traffic regulations are no good—then I get impatient and tell him to shut up. And that's all the birth-control statutes are: a series of regulations to make the reproductive traffic of the human race flow more efficiently."

The voices from the entrance hall stopped abruptly. They heard Marian make a peculiar noise, halfway between a squeal and a scream. Both men leaped to their feet and ran through the archway to her.

She was in the foyer, standing beside Bruce Robertson. Her eyes were shut and she had one hand on the wall as if it alone kept her from falling.

"I'm sorry I upset her, Stew," the book illustrator said rapidly. His face was very pale. "You see, I want to adopt Lisa. Frank Tyler told me what happened today."

"*You?* You want to— But you're a bachelor!"

"Yes, but I'm in a five-child bracket income. I can adopt Lisa if I can prove that I can give her as good a home as a married couple might. Well, I can. All I want is for her last name to be changed legally to Robertson—I don't care what name she uses in school or with her friends—and she'll go on staying here, with me providing for her maintenance. The FPB would consider that the best possible home."

Raley stared at Boettiger. The lawyer nodded. "It would. Besides that, if the natural parents express any wishes for a feasible adoptive situation, the weight of administrative action tends to be thrown in that direction. But what would you be getting out of that, young man?"

"I'd be getting a child—officially," Robertson told him. "I'd be getting a kid I could talk about, boast about, when other men boast about theirs. I'm sick and tired of being a no-child bachelor. I want to be *somebody*."

"But you might want to get married one day," Raley said, putting his arm about his wife, who had let a long breath out and turned to him. "You might want to get married and have children of your own."

"No, I wouldn't," Bruce Robertson said in a low voice. "Please don't pass this on, but there's amaurotic idiocy in my hereditary background. The only woman who'd ever marry me would be a sterile one. I doubt that I'll ever get married, but I certainly won't ever have kids. This—this is my only chance."

"Oh, darling," Marian sobbed happily in Raley's arms. "It will work. It really will work!"

"All I ask," the book illustrator went on uncertainly, "is the privilege of coming here once in a while, to kind of see Lisa and see what's going on with her."

"Once in a while!" Raley roared. "You can come every night. After all, you'll be like a member of the family. *Like* a member of the family? You'll *be* a member of the family; man, you'll *be* the family!"

... about William Tenn

William Tenn says "I've wanted to be a writer ever since I read a story in the first-grade spelling book. From time to time, I've wanted other professions, too—medicine, engineering, the stage— and have even pried about in the institutions that purport to prepare for them, but always with the clear personal understanding that they would merely fill up the time between stories and novels.

"I went to several colleges, but never got within any measurable distance of a degree. The only things I didn't study at all were literature and writing—because I considered them, like courses in breathing and eating, superfluous. Recently, however, I've come to regret my feelings of superiority in this area; there are quite a few things I wish I had studied and am getting around to even now.

"Since the war I've been a professional writer, taking time out occasionally in the leaner months to run my own sales-promotion business, go to sea as a purser, wait on tables, demonstrate cooking appliances to women in department stores, work as a stickman in a small-time gambling joint, do a minor bit of comic acting on television, act as nursemaid to several thousand rare tropical fish, interview suburban housewives in the interests of market research on washing-machine detergents, and even—when times got really tough—going so far as to become a magazine editor myself."

Mr. Tenn was born in London in 1920. He is unmarried and lives in New York City. What time is free from writing stories about the future, he spends studying ancient Greek.

OTHER BALLANTINE SCIENCE FICTION